FH

C90 0989702

D0832664

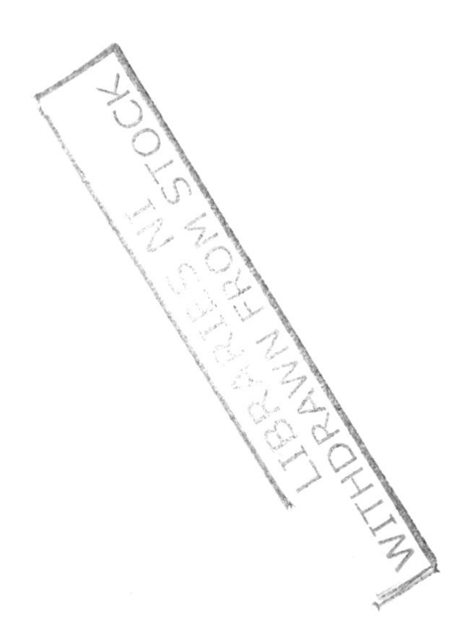
LIBRARIES NI
WITHDRAWN FROM STOCK

She sighed, then put down the pen. "This isn't going to work if you keep flirting with me."

"I'm not flirting with you, Marnie. If I was flirting with you, you'd know it."

"That," she waved a finger between them, "was definitely flirting."

"No. *This* is flirting." He got up again and approached her desk, then placed his hands on the oak surface and leaned over until their faces were inches apart.

"You are a beautiful, intoxicating, infuriating woman," he whispered, his voice a low, sensual growl, "and I can't stop thinking about you. And I love the way you look today. All… unfettered. Untamed."

Heat washed over her body. "Okay." Her words shook and she drew in a breath to steady herself. "Yes, that…that was flirting."

He smiled, held her gaze a moment longer, then retreated to the chair. "Glad we got that settled."

Settled? If anything, things between them had become more unsettled. Jack Knight. The enemy. In more ways than one.

Dear Reader

Mother's Day has been a tough holiday for me to celebrate in the years since I lost my own mother. The first couple of years I didn't want to do anything to acknowledge the day, because it was too painful to be reminded that I didn't have my mom around to call, to talk to, to visit with. I would just ignore the holiday and spend it like any other Sunday.

In the last two years or so I've had a change of heart. I've started to look at Mother's Day as a way to celebrate not just my amazing children, but everything that nurtures and fulfils us. The only thing I want for Mother's Day is a trip to the garden centre, so I can pick up my spring flowers and spend the day in the garden, weeding, pruning and renewing areas that have been long neglected. Then I can step back and see the flowers bloom day after day, giving me a little happy reminder of Mother's Day for months afterwards. To me, it's like a long visit from my own mother when I walk outside and see the impatiens and pansies waving in the breeze. And because my kids have helped me plant and tend them, it gives me some special time with each of them as well.

I hope you enjoy this mother-daughter story, and the special bond that Marnie has with her mom. And I also hope that you, dear reader, have a wonderful Mother's Day, and find a way to take a peek at Mother Nature's beautiful gifts each and every day.

Shirley

THE MATCHMAKER'S HAPPY ENDING

BY
SHIRLEY JUMP

First published in Great Britain 2013
by Mills & Boon, an imprint of Harlequin (UK) Limited.
Harlequin (UK) Limited, Eton House, 18-24 Paradise Road,
Richmond, Surrey TW9 1SR

ISBN: 978 0 263 23474 9

Harlequin (UK) policy is to use papers that are natural, renewable and recyclable products and made from wood grown in sustainable forests. The logging and manufacturing process conform to the legal environmental regulations of the country of origin.

Printed and bound in Great Britain
by CPI Antony Rowe, Chippenham, Wiltshire

New York Times bestselling author **Shirley Jump** didn't have the will-power to diet, nor the talent to master under-eye concealer, so she bowed out of a career in television and opted instead for a career where she could be paid to eat at her desk—writing. At first, seeking revenge on her children for their grocery store tantrums, she sold embarrassing essays about them to anthologies. However, it wasn't enough to feed her growing addiction to writing funny. So she turned to the world of romance novels, where messes are (usually) cleaned up before The End. In the worlds Shirley gets to create and control, the children listen to their parents, the husbands always remember holidays, and the housework is magically done by elves. Though she's thrilled to see her books in stores around the world, Shirley mostly writes because it gives her an excuse to avoid cleaning the toilets and helps feed her shoe habit.

To learn more, visit her website at www.shirleyjump.com

Books by Shirley Jump:

MISTLETOE KISSES WITH THE BILLIONAIRE
RETURN OF THE LAST McKENNA*
HOW THE PLAYBOY GOT SERIOUS*
ONE DAY TO FIND A HUSBAND*
THE PRINCESS TEST
HOW TO LASSO A COWBOY
IF THE RED SLIPPER FITS
VEGAS PREGNANCY SURPRISE
BEST MAN SAYS I DO

**The McKenna Brothers* trilogy

To Mom. I miss you every day.

CHAPTER ONE

MARNIE FRANKLIN LEFT her thirtieth wedding of the year, with aching feet, flower petals in her hair and a satisfied smile on her face. She'd done it. Again.

From behind the wide glass and brass doors of Boston's Park Plaza hotel, the newly married Mr. and Mrs. Andrew Corliss waved and shouted their thanks. "We owe it all to you, Marnie!" Andrew called. A geeky but lovable guy who tended toward neon colored ties that were knotted too tight around his skinny neck, Andrew had been one of her best success stories. Internet millionaire, now married to an energetic, friendly woman who loved him for his mind—and their mutual affection for difficult Sudoku puzzles.

"You're welcome! May you have a long and happy life together." Marnie gave them a smile, then turned to the street and waited while a valet waved up one of the half dozen waiting cabs outside the hotel. Exhaustion weighed on Marnie's shoulders, despite the two cups of coffee she'd downed at the reception. A light rain had started, adding a chill to the late spring air. The always busy Boston traffic passed the hotel in a *swoosh-swoosh* of tires on damp pavement, a melody highlighted by the honking of horns, the constant music of a city. She loved this city, she really did, but there were days—like today—when she wished she lived somewhere quiet. Like the other side of the moon.

Her phone rang as she opened the taxi's door and told the driver her address. She pressed mute, sending the call straight to voice mail. That was the trouble with being on the top of her field—there was no room for a holiday or vacation. She'd become one of Boston's most successful matchmakers, and that meant everyone who wanted a happy ending called her, looking for true love.

Something she didn't believe in herself.

An irony she couldn't tell her clients. Couldn't admit she'd never fallen in love, and had given up on the emotion after one too many failed relationships. She couldn't tell people that the matchmaker had no faith in a match for herself. So she poured herself into her job and kept a bright smile on her face whenever she told her clients that they could have that happy ending, too.

She'd seen the fairy tale ending happen for other people, but a part of Marnie wondered if she'd missed her one big chance to have a happily-ever-after. She was almost thirty, and had yet to meet Mr. Right. Only a few heartbreaker Mr. Wrongs. At least with her job, she had some control over the outcome, which was the way Marnie preferred the things in her life. Controlled, predictable. The phone rang again, like a punctuation mark to the end of her thoughts.

In front of her, the cabbie pulled away from the curb, at the same time fiddling with the GPS on the dash. Must be a new driver, Marnie decided, and grabbed her phone to answer the call. "This is Marnie. How can I help you make a match?"

"You need to stop working, dear, and find your own Mr. Right."

Her mother. Who meant well, but who thought Marnie's personal life should take precedence over everything else in the universe. "Hi, Ma. What are you doing up so late on a Friday night?"

"Worrying about my single daughter. And why she's working on a Friday night. Again."

The GPS announced a left turn, a little late for the distracted cab driver, who jerked the wheel to the left and jerked Marnie to one side, too. She gave him a glare in the rearview mirror, but he ignored it. The noxious fumes of Boston exhaust filled the interior, or maybe that was the bad ventilation system in the cab. The car had seen better days, heck, better decades, if the duct tape on the scarred vinyl seats was any indication.

"You should be out on a date of your own," Marnie countered to her mother.

"Oh, I'm too old for that foolishness," Helen said. "Besides, your father hasn't been gone that long."

"Three years, Ma." Marnie lowered her voice to a sympathetic tone. Dad's heart attack had taken them all by surprise. One day he'd been there, grinning and heading out the door, the next he'd been a shell of himself, and then…gone. "It's okay to move on."

"So, what are you doing on Sunday?" her mother said, instead of responding to Marnie's advice, a surefire Helen tactic. Change the topic from anything difficult. Marnie's parents had been the type who avoided the hard stuff, swept it under the rug. To them, the world had been a perpetually sunny place, even when evidence to the contrary dropped a big gray shadow in their way.

A part of Marnie wanted to keep things that way for her mother, to protect Helen, who had been through so much.

"I wanted to have you and your sisters over for

brunch after church," Ma said. "I could serve that coffee cake you love and..."

As her mother talked about the menu, Marnie murmured agreement, and reviewed her To Do list in her head. She had three appointments with new clients early in the morning tomorrow, one afternoon bachelor meet and greet to host, then her company's Saturday night speed date event—

"Did you hear what I said?" her mother cut in.

"Sorry, Ma. The connection faded." Or her brain, but she didn't say that.

The cab driver fiddled again with the GPS, pushing buttons to zoom in or out, Marnie wasn't sure. He seemed flustered and confused. She leaned forward. "Just take a left up here," she said to him. "Onto Boylston. Then a right on Harvard."

The cabbie nodded.

And went straight.

"Hey, you missed the turn." Damn it. Was the man that green? Marnie gave up the argument and sat back against the seat. After the long day she'd had, the delay was more welcome than annoying. Especially to her feet, which were already complaining about the upcoming three-flight walk upstairs to her condo. She loved the brick building she lived in, with its tree-lined street located within walking distance of the quirky neighborhood of Coolidge Corner. But there were days when living on the third floor—despite the nice view of the park across the street—was exhausting after a long day. Right this second, she'd do about anything for an elevator and a massage chair.

"I said you should wear a dress to brunch on Sunday," her mother said, "because I'm inviting Stella Hargrove's grandson. He's single and—"

"Wouldn't it be nicer just to visit with you and my sisters, Ma? That way, we can all catch up, which we never seem to get enough time to do. A guy would end up being a fifth wheel." Marnie pressed a finger to her temple, but it did little to ward off the impending headache. A headache her sister Erica would say she brought on herself because she never confronted her mother and instead placated and deferred. Instead of saying *Ma, don't fix me up,* she'd fallen back on making nice instead. Marnie was the middle sister, the peacemaker, even if sometimes that peace came with the price of a lot of aspirin. "Besides, if I want a date, I have a whole file of handsome men to go through."

"Yet you haven't done that at all. You keep working and working and…oh, I just worry about you, honey."

Ever since their father had died, Helen had made her three children her top—and only—priority. No matter how many times Marnie and her sisters had encouraged their mother to take a class, pick up a hobby, go on a trip, she demurred, and refocused the conversation on her girls. What her mother needed was an outside life. Something else to focus on. Something like a…

Man.

Marnie smacked herself in the head. For goodness sake, she was a professional matchmaker. Why had she never thought to fix up her mother? Marnie had made great matches for both of her sisters. Oldest sister Kat got married to her match two years ago, and Erica was in a steady relationship with a man Marnie had introduced her to last month. Despite that, Marnie had never thought about doing the same for her widowed mother. First thing tomorrow morning, she would cull her files and find a selection of distinguished, older men. Who appreciated women with a penchant for meddling.

"I'll be there for brunch on Sunday, Ma, I promise," Marnie said, noting the cabbie again messing with the GPS. "Maybe next time we can invite Stella's grandson. Okay?"

Her mother sighed. "Okay. But if you want me to give him your number or give you his..."

"I know who to call." Marnie started to say something else when the cabbie swore, stomped on his brakes—

And rear-ended the car in front of him. Marnie jerked forward, the seatbelt cutting across her sternum but saving her from plowing into the plexiglass partition. She let out an oomph, winced at the sharp pain that erupted in her chest, while the cabbie let out a stream of curses.

"What was that sound?" Helen asked. "It sounded like a boom. Did something fall? Did you hit something?"

"It's, uh, nothing. I gotta go, Ma," Marnie said, and after a breath, then another, the pain in her chest eased. "See you tomorrow." She hung up the phone, then unbuckled, and climbed out of the yellow cab. The hood had crumpled, and steam poured from the engine in angry gusts. The cabbie clambered out of the taxi. He let out another long stream of curses, a few in a language other than English, then started pacing back and forth between the driver's side door and the impact site, holding his head and muttering.

The accordioned trunk of a silver sports car was latched onto the taxi's hood. A tall, dark, handsome, and angry man stood beside the idling luxury car. He shouted at the cab driver, who threw up his hands and feigned non-understanding, as if he'd suddenly lost all knowledge of the English language.

Marnie grabbed her purse from the car, and walked

over to the man. One of those attractive, business types, she thought, noting his dark pinstriped suit, loosened tie, white button-down with the top button undone. A five o'clock shadow dusted his strong jaw, and gave his dark hair and blue eyes a sexy air. The matchmaker in her recognized the kind of good-looking man always in demand with her clients. But the woman in her—

Well, she noticed him on an entirely different level, one that sent a shimmer of heat down her veins and sped up her pulse. Something she hadn't felt in so long, she'd begun to wonder if she'd ever meet another man who interested her.

Either way, Mr. Suit and Tie looked like a lawyer or something. The last thing she needed was a rich, uptight man with control issues. She'd met enough of them that she could pick his type out of the thousands of people in the stands at Fenway on opening day.

"Is everyone okay?" she asked.

The cab driver nodded. Mr. Suit and Tie shot him a scowl, then turned to Marnie. His features softened. "Yeah. I'm fine," he said. "You?"

"I'm okay. Just a little shaken up."

"Good." He held her gaze for a moment longer, then turned on the cabbie. "Didn't you see that red light? Where'd you get your license? A vending machine?"

The cabbie just shook his head, as if he didn't understand a word.

Mr. Suit and Tie let out a curse and shook his head, then pivoted back to Marnie. "What were you thinking, riding around this city with a maniacal cab driver?"

"It's not like I get a resume and insurance record handed to me before I get in a taxi," she said. "Now, I understand you're frustrated, but—"

"I'm *beyond* frustrated. This has been a hell of a day.

With one hell of a bad ending." He shot the cab driver another glare, but the man had already skulked back to his car and climbed behind the wheel. "Wait! What are you doing?"

"I'm not doing any—" Then she heard the sound of metal groaning, and tires squealing, and realized Mr. Suit and Tie wasn't talking to her—but to the cab driver who had just hit and run. The yellow car disappeared around the corner in a noisy, clanking cloud of smoke.

In the distance, she heard the rising sound of sirens, which meant one of the people living in the apartments lining the street must have already called 9-1-1. Not soon enough.

Mr. Suit and Tie cursed under his breath. "Great. That's all I needed today."

"I'm sorry about that." Marnie stepped to the corner and put up her hand for a passing cab. "Well, good luck. Hope you get it straightened out and your night gets better."

"Hey! You can't leave. You're my witness."

"Listen, I'm exhausted and I just want to get home." She raised her arm higher, waving her hand, hoping to see at least one available cab. Nothing. Her feet screamed in protest. Soon as she got home, she was burning these shoes. "I'll give you my number. Call me for my statement." She fished in her purse for a business card, and held it out.

He ignored the card. "I need you to stay."

"And I need to get home." She waved harder, but the lone cab that passed her didn't stop. "This is Boston. Why aren't there any cabs?"

"Celtics game is just getting over," the man said. "They're probably all over at the Garden."

"Great." She lowered her arm, then thought of the

ten-block hike home. Not fun in high heels. Even less fun after an eighteen-hour day, the last four spent dancing and socializing. She should have drunk an entire pot of coffee.

"I'll make you a deal," the man said. "I'll give you a lift if you can wait until I've finished making the accident report. Then you can give your statement and kill two birds with one stone."

She hesitated. "I don't know. I'm really tired."

"Stay for just a bit more. After tonight, you'll never have to see me again." He grinned.

He had a nice smile. An echoing smile curved across her face. She glanced down the street in the direction of her condo and thought of the soft bed waiting for her there. She weighed that against walking home. Option two made her feet hurt ten times more. *Stupid shoes.*

She glanced back at the misshapen silver car. "You're sure you can drive me home? In that?"

"It runs. It's just got a little junk in the trunk." He grinned. "Sorry. Bad joke."

A laugh escaped her and eased some of the tension in her shoulders, the pain in her feet. "Even a bad joke sounds good right now." No cabs appeared, and that settled the decision for her. "Okay, I'll wait."

Not that it was going to be a hardship to wait with a view like that. This guy could have been a cover model. Whew. Hot, hot, hot. She should get his contact information. She had at least a dozen clients who would be—

You're always working.

Marnie could hear her mother's voice in her head. *Take some time off. Have some fun. Date a guy for yourself. Don't be so serious and buttoned up all the time.*

What no one seemed to understand was this buttoned-up approach had fueled Marnie's success.

She'd seen how a laissez-faire approach to business could destroy a company and refused to repeat those mistakes herself. A distraction like Mr. Suit and Tie would only derail her, something she couldn't afford.

The man opened the passenger's side door. "Have a seat. You look like you've had a trying day. And I know how that feels."

She sank into the leather seat, kicked off her shoes and let the platform heels tumble to the sidewalk. The man came to stand beside her, leaning against the rear passenger door. He had the look of a man comfortable in his own skin, at ease with the world. Confident, sexy, but not overly so. A hot combination, especially with the suit and tie. Her stance toward him softened.

"You're right. I have had a long, trying day myself." She put out her hand. "Let's try this again. I'm Marnie Franklin."

"Jack Knight."

The name rang a bell, but the connection flitted away before she could grasp it because when he took her hand in his, a delicious spark ran through her, down her arm. If she hadn't been seated, she might have jumped back in surprise. In her business, she shook hands with dozens of men in the course of a week. None had ever sent that little...zing through her. Maybe exhaustion had lowered her defenses. Or maybe the accident had shaken her up more than she thought. She released his hand, and brushed the hair out of her eyes, if only to keep from touching him again.

The police arrived, two officers who looked like they'd rather be going for a root canal than taking another accident report in the dent and ding city of Boston. For the next ten minutes Marnie and Jack answered questions. After the police were gone, Jack turned to her. "Thanks for staying. You made a stressful day much better."

"Glad to help."

Jack bent down and picked up the black heels she'd kicked onto the sidewalk when she'd sat in his car. He handed them to Marnie, the twin heels dangling from his index finger by their strappy backs. In his strong, capable hands, the fancy shoes looked even more delicate. "Your shoes, Cinderella." He gave her a wink, and that zing rushed through her a second time.

"I'm far from Cinderella." She bent and slipped on the damnable slingbacks. Pretty, but painful. "More like the not-so-evil stepmother, trying to fix up all the stepsisters with princes."

His smile had a dash of sexy, a glimmer of a tease. "Every woman deserves to be Cinderella at least once in her life."

"Maybe so, *if* she believes in fairy tales and magic mice."

She worked in the business of helping people fall in love, and had given up on the fairy tale herself a long time ago. Over the years, she'd become, if anything, more cautious, less willing to dip a toe in the romance pool. When she'd started matchmaking she'd been starry eyed, hopeful. But now…

Now she had a lot of years of reality beneath her and the stars had faded from her vision. She knew her business had suffered as a consequence. Somehow she needed to restore her belief in the very thing she touted to her clients—the existence of true love.

Jack shut her door and came around to the driver's side. The car started with a soft purr. "Where to?"

She gave him her address, and he put the car in gear. She settled into the luxury seat. The dark leather hugged her body, warm and easy. Damn. She needed to step outside the basic car model box because sitting in this sedan made it pretty easy to fall for the whole Cinderella fantasy. It wasn't a white horse, but it was a giant step closer to a royal ride. Having a good looking prince beside her helped feed that fantasy, too.

"I'm sorry for being grumpy earlier. That accident was the icing on a tough day. Thanks again for staying and talking to the cops for me," he said. "I can't believe you remembered all those details about the driver."

She shrugged. "My father used to make me do that. Whenever we went someplace, he made sure I noticed the waiter's name or the cab driver's ID. He'd have me recite the address or license plate or some other detail. He said you never knew when doing that would come in handy, and he was right." She could almost hear her father's voice in her ear. *Watch the details, Daisy-doo, because you never know when they'll matter.* He'd rarely called her Marnie, almost always Daisy-doo, because of her love for the flowers. Kat had been Kitty, Erica had been Chatterbug. Marnie missed hearing her father's wisdom, the way he lovingly teased his daughters. "Besides, the cab driver had his hands on the GPS more than the steering wheel, and that made me doubly nervous. If I could have, I would have jumped in the driver's seat and taken the wheel myself."

He chuckled. "Nice to meet a fellow control freak."

"Me? I'm not a control freak." She wrinkled her nose. "Okay, maybe I am. A little. But in my house, things were a little…crazy when I was a kid and someone had to take the reins."

"Let me guess. You're the oldest? An only?"

"The middle kid, but only younger than the oldest by nine months."

"Oh, so not just the driver, but the peacemaker, too?" He tossed her a grin.

He'd nailed her, in a few words. "Do you read personality trait books in your spare time or something?"

"Nah. I'm just in a business where it's essential to be able to read people, quickly, and well."

"Me, too. Though sometimes you don't like what you read."

"True." Jack glanced over at her, his blue eyes holding her features for a long moment before he returned his attention to the road. "So, Cinderella, what has made you so jaded?"

The conversational detour jolted her. She shifted in her seat. "Not jaded…realistic."

"Well, that makes two of us. I find, in my line of work, that realism is a must."

The amber glow of the street lights and the soft white light coming from the dash outlined his lean, defined profile with a soft edge. Despite the easy tone of his words, something in them hinted at a past that hadn't been easy. Maybe a bad breakup, or a bitter divorce? Either way, despite the zing, she wasn't interested in cleaning up someone else's baggage. *Stick to impersonal topics, Marnie.*

His cell phone started to ring, and the touchscreen in the center of his dash lit up with the word Dad. "Do you mind if I answer this?" Jack asked. "If I don't, he'll just keep calling."

She chuckled and waved toward the screen. "Go right ahead. I totally understand."

Jack leaned forward, pressed a button on the screen, then sat back again. "Hey, Dad, what's up? And before you say a word, you're on speaker, so don't blurt out any family secrets or embarrassing stories."

"You got someone in the car with you?" said a deep, amused voice on the other end. "Someone pretty, I hope."

Jack glanced at Marnie. A slow smile stole across his face and a quiver ran through her. "Yes, someone very pretty. So be on your best behavior."

His father chuckled. "That's no fun. The only thing that gets me out of bed in the morning is the potential for bad behavior."

Beside her, Jack rolled his eyes and grinned. *Parents,* he mouthed.

Seemed she wasn't the only one with a troublesome parent. Jack handled his father with a nice degree of love and humor. That tender touch raised her esteem for him, and had her looking past the suit and tie. Intriguing man. Almost...intoxicating.

She didn't have time, or room, in her life for being intrigued by a man, though, especially since her business took nearly every spare moment. Even one as handsome as him.

She could almost hear her mother screaming in disagreement, but Marnie knew her business and herself. If she got involved with someone right now, it would be a distraction. Maybe down the road, when her business and life were more settled...

Someday when?

She'd been saying "someday" for years. And had to find the right moment—or the right man—to make her open her heart to love.

"I called because I was wondering when you'd be home," Jack's father was saying. "You work more hours than the President, for God's sake."

Marnie bit back a laugh. It could have been her conversation with her mother a little while ago. She half expected his father to schedule a blind date brunch, too.

"I'm on my way." Jack flicked a glance at the dashboard clock. "Give me twenty minutes. Did you eat?"

"Yeah. Sandwiches. *Again.* Lord knows you don't have anything in that refrigerator of yours besides beer and moldy takeout."

"Because I'm never there to eat."

"Exactly." Jack's father cleared his throat. "I have an idea. Maybe…you should bring your pretty companion home for a—"

"Hey, no embarrassing statements, remember?"

His father chuckled. "Okay, okay. Drive safe."

Jack told his father he'd be home soon, then said goodbye and disconnected the call. "Sorry about that," Jack said to Marnie. "My dad is…needy sometimes. Even though it's been a few years since he got divorced, it's like he's been lost."

"My mother is the same way. She calls me every five minutes to make sure I'm eating my vegetables, wearing sunscreen and not working too much."

He chuckled. "Sounds like we have the same parent. Ever since my dad sold his house, he's been living with me, while he tries to figure out if he wants to stay in Boston or high-tail it for sunny Florida. He thinks that means he should comment on everything I do and every piece of furniture in my apartment."

"And what is or isn't in your fridge." Marnie's mom stopped by Marnie's condo almost every Sunday after church, but less to visit than to do a responsible child check. *You need more vegetables,* her mother would say. Or *you should cook for yourself more often.* And the best, *if you had a man in your life, you wouldn't have to do that.* Marnie loved her mother, but had realized a long time ago that a mother's love could be… invasive. "I get the whole you should make more time for homecooked meals and a personal life lecture on a weekly basis. I think my mother forgets how many hours I work. The last thing I want to do when I get home is whip up a platter of lasagna."

"I think they go to school for that," Jack said. "How to Bug Your Adult Kids 101."

She laughed. It did sound like they had the same parent. "Maybe you should get your dad involved in something else, something that keeps him too busy to focus on you. There are all kinds of singles events for people his age. Some of them are dates in disguise, get-togethers centered around hobbies, like cooking or pets," Marnie said, unable to stop work talk from invading every second of her day. My lord, she was a compulsive matchmaker. And one who needed to take her own advice. First thing tomorrow, she was going to look into dates for Ma and someday soon, she'd nicely tell her mother to butt out.

Yeah, right. Marnie had yet to do that to anyone, especially her mother. But she could tell others what to do. *That* she excelled at, according to her sisters.

Jack nodded. "I tried that before, years ago, but it didn't go so well. But you're right—maybe if I try again, now that some time has passed since all that upheaval, my dad will be more open to doing some activities, especially ones that get him dating again."

"And if he meets someone else—"

"He won't have time to worry about my fridge or my hours." Jack laughed. "Ah, such a devious plan we've concocted."

"As long as it works." She grinned.

Jack turned onto Marnie's street. A flicker of disappointment ran through her as the ride came to an end. "It's the fourth one on the right," she said. "With the flowers out front."

Invite him in? Or call it a night?

He slowed the car, then stopped at her building's entrance. "Nice looking place. I love these brick buildings from the early 1900s. It's always nice to see the architecture get preserved when the building gets repurposed. Not every owner appreciates history like that."

"Me, too. Coming home is like stepping into history." She smiled, then put out her hand. Impersonal, business-like. "Well, thank you for the ride."

That zing ran through her again when his large hand enfolded hers. For a second, she had the crazy thought of yanking on his hand, pulling him across the car, and kissing him. His broad chest against hers, his lips dancing around her mouth, his hands—

Wow. She needed to sleep more or get extra potassium or something.

"It was the least I could do after you stayed," Jack was saying. He released her hand. Darn. "Especially after you had a long day yourself."

Focus on the words he's speaking, not the fantasy. She jerked her gaze away from his mouth. "It was no trouble."

He grinned. "You said that already."

"Oh, well, I'm just really…tired."

"Yeah, me, too. I had a long day, made longer by someone who dropped the ball on some important paperwork. I got everything back on track, but…what a day." He ran a hand through his hair, displacing the dark locks. "Anyway, I'm sorry again about losing my temper back there."

"I would have done the same thing if my trunk looked like an origami project," she said.

He glanced in the rearview mirror and shrugged off the damaged rear. "It gives my insurance agent something to do."

She laughed. "True. Anyway, thanks again. Have a good night."

"You, too." He reached for her before she got out of the car, a light, quick touch on her arm. But still enough to send heat searing along her skin. "Would you like to go get a cup of coffee or a drink? We could sit around and complain about our jobs, our meddling parents, bad cab drivers and whatever else we can think of?"

A part of her wanted to say yes, but the realistic part piped up, reminding her of the time and her To Do list, and her no-men-for-the-foreseeable-future resolve. Besides, there was something about that zing, something that told her if she caved, she'd be lost, swept in a tsunami. The mere thought terrified her. "I can't. It's late. And I have an early day tomorrow."

"On Saturday?"

She raised one shoulder, let it drop. "My job is a 24/7 kind of thing."

He chuckled. "Mine, too. And even though every year I vow to work less and play more…"

"You don't."

He nodded.

"Me, too." Because work was easier than confronting the reasons why she worked too much. Because work was easier than taking a chance on love. Work she could control, depend upon. Love, not so much. But she didn't say any of that. She released the door handle, and shifted to face him.

Despite the fear, she didn't want to leave. Right

now, with Jack looking at her like that, his eyes lit by the street light above and his strong jaw cast in a dark shadow, her resistance was at an all-time low. Desire pulsed in her veins. She wished she *had* dragged him across the car and kissed him silly when she'd had the chance. So she delayed leaving a bit longer.

"What do you do for work that keeps you busy late into the day and also on weekends?" She put a finger to her lip and gave him a flirty smile. "Let me guess. Lawyer?"

"Hell, no." He glanced down. "Oh, I get it. Pinstripe suit, power tie. Screams waiting to sue to you?"

"Well, if the Brooks Brothers fits…"

His smile widened, ending with a dimple. *Oh, God.* Dimples. She'd always been a sucker for them.

"I'm…an investor," Jack said. "Of sorts."

"Of sorts?"

"I buy and sell businesses. I find ones that need a cash infusion, and if I think they're viable, I invest. If I think they're not, I buy them and either sell them again or break up the pieces and sell it off."

A shiver ran down her back. The leather seemed to chafe now, not comfort. "You're…a corporate raider?"

"I'm a little nicer than that. And I tend to work with small to medium-sized businesses, not giant Goliaths."

The connection fused in her mind. His job. His name.

Jack Knight. Owner of Knight Enterprises. A "business investor"—a euphemism for his true identity. Jack Knight was a vulture. Feeding off the carcasses of desperate business owners.

It had to have been the exhaustion of the day that had kept her from putting the pieces together until now. How could she have misread all the clues?

And to think she'd wanted to kiss him five minutes

ago. She bristled. "The size doesn't matter to the company that gets sold off, or taken over, or destroyed in the process of that kind of 'help.'"

"I must have given you the wrong impression. There's more to it—"

"No, there really isn't. You destroy people's companies, and their lives." The words sprang to life in her throat, fueled by exhaustion, shock, and surprised even Marnie with their vehemence. She never did this, never showed outrage, never yelled. Jack Knight had brought out this other side of her, with a roar. "Do you even think about what happens to those people after you swoop in and tear their company to shreds? They spent their lives building those companies, and in an instant, you take it all away. And for what? A bottom line? A few more dollars in your pocket? Another sports car for the collection?" She let out a gust, then grabbed the door handle. It stuck, then yielded, and fresh night air washed over her. She'd gotten distracted, by a dimple and a zing. *Idiot.* "Goodnight."

"Wait. What did—"

She shut the door, cutting off his words. She'd confronted him, told him off, and told herself it felt good to finally say what she should say, exactly when she was supposed to say it. Jack idled in the space for a moment, then finally, he drove away, swallowed by the night.

Disappointment hit her first. If only she'd kissed him. If only she'd let herself get talked into that cup of coffee.

If only he'd been someone other than Jack Knight.

Then righteous indignation rose in her chest. He was the one at fault, not her. He was the one who had ruined her father's company, not her. If she'd told him what she really wanted to say to him, if she'd really let the confrontation loose, she'd have resorted to some very unlady-like behavior, and she refused to give him that satisfaction. Jack Knight didn't deserve it, not after what he had done to her father.

So she had said goodnight, got out of Cinderella's carriage, and went back to the real world, where princes didn't come along very often, and there were no mice to do the work for her.

CHAPTER TWO

"ARE YOU GOING to admit I was right?" Marnie whispered to her mother. They were standing to the side of the private dining room of an upscale Boston restaurant on a sunny Saturday afternoon. Soft jazz music filled the air, accented by the rise and fall of a dozen human voices.

A blush filled Helen's cheeks, making her look ten years younger. She had her chestnut hair up tonight, which elongated her neck and offset her deep green eyes. The dark blue dress she'd worn skimmed her calves, and defined the hourglass shape she'd maintained all her life, even after giving birth to three children. Coupled with the light in her eyes and the smile on her face, Helen looked prettier than ever, and far younger than her fifty-eight years.

"Yes, you were right, daughter dear," Helen whispered back. "How'd I get such a smart child?"

"You gave me great genes." Marnie glanced over the room. Cozy and intimate, the private dining space offered a prime location, great parking and an outstanding menu, making it perfect for Matchmaking by Marnie meet and greets. In her experience, full and happy stomachs equaled happy people who then struck up conversations.

Today, she'd invited ten bachelors to meet her mother, and set up a buffet of finger foods on the far right side of the room. While they noshed on chicken satay and mini eggrolls, Helen circulated. Three days ago, when Marnie and Erica had proposed the idea of a mixer to Helen, she'd refused, insisting she didn't need to be fixed up, and didn't want to be, but after a while, she'd relented and agreed to "put in an appearance."

That appearance had lasted more than an hour now. Once the first man talked to Helen, and two more joined the conversation, Marnie had watched her mother transform into a giggling schoolgirl, flattered by all the sudden attention. Marnie made sure each bachelor got equal time, then stepped back and allowed the pieces to fall where they may. She'd paved the way, then let Mother Nature finish giving directions.

"So," Marnie said, leaning in closer so they wouldn't be overheard, "is there one man in particular who you like the most?"

Pink bloomed in Helen's cheeks. "Do you see the one standing by the bar?"

"The tall man with the gray hair?" Marnie and Erica had interviewed so many eligible gentlemen in the fifty- to sixty-plus age range that some of them had become a bit of a blur. She didn't remember the details of this man, only that he had impressed her during the group interviews.

"His name's Dan. He's retired from his landscaping business, hates to golf, but loves to watch old movies." Her mother grinned, and in that smile, Marnie could see the energy of a new relationship already blossoming. "And, you'll never guess what his favorite movie is."

Marnie put a finger to her lip. "Hmm...*Casablanca?*"

Helen nodded. "Just like me. We like the same kind

of wine, the same kind of music, and both of us love to travel."

"Sounds like a match made in heaven." Marnie grinned. "Or a match made by a daughter who knows her mother very well."

Helen chuckled. "Well, I wouldn't say it's a perfect match…yet, but it's got potential. Big potential. Now, if only we could find someone for you." Helen brushed a lock of hair off Marnie's forehead. "You deserve to be happy, sweetheart."

"I am happy." And she was, Marnie told herself. She had a business she loved, a purpose to her life, and a family that might annoy her sometimes, but had always been her personal rock. She gave her mother a quick hug, then headed for the front of the room, waiting until everyone's attention swiveled toward her before speaking. She noticed Dan's gaze remained on her mother, while Helen snuck quick glances back in his direction, like two teenagers at a football game.

"I wanted to thank you all for coming today, and if you weren't lucky enough to be chosen by our amazing and beautiful bachelorette," Marnie gestured toward her mother, who waved off the compliment, "don't worry. My goal at Matchmaking by Marnie is to give everyone a happy ending. So work with me, and I promise, I'll help you find your perfect match."

The bachelors thanked her, and began to file out of the room. Dan lingered, chatting with Marnie's mother. She laughed and flirted, seeming like an entirely different person, the person she used to be years and years ago. Marnie sent up a silent prayer of gratitude. Her mother had been lonely for a long time, and it was nice to see her happy again.

The waitstaff began taking away the dishes and

cleaning the tables. Marnie gathered her purse and jacket, then touched her mother on the arm. "I'm going to get going, Ma. Call me later, okay?"

Her mother promised, then returned her attention to Dan. The two of them were still chatting when Marnie headed out of the restaurant. She stood by the valet counter, waiting for the valet to return with her car, when a black sports car pulled up to the station. The passenger's side window slid down. "You're like a bad penny, turning up everywhere I go."

The voice took a second to register in her mind. It had been a couple weeks since she'd last heard that deep baritone, and in the busy-ness of working twenty-hour days, she'd nearly forgotten the encounter.

Almost.

Late at night, when she was alone and the day had gone quiet, her mind would wander and she'd wonder what might have happened if he'd been someone other than Jack Knight and she'd agreed to that cup of coffee. Then she would jerk herself back to reality.

Jack Knight was the worst kind of corporate vermin—and the last kind of man she should be thinking about late at night, or any time. Of all the people in the city of Boston, how did she end up running into him twice?

She bent down and peered inside the car. Jack grinned back at her. He had a hell of a smile, she'd give him that. The kind of smile that charmed and tempted, all at once. Yeah, like a snake. "Speaking of bad pennies," she said, "what are you doing here?"

"Picking up my father." His head disappeared from view, and a moment later, he had stepped out of the car and crossed to her. He had on khakis and a pale blue button-down shirt, the wrinkled bottom slightly untucked, the top two buttons undone, as if he was just knocking off after putting in a full day of work, even on a Saturday. He looked sexy, approachable. If she ignored his name and his job, that was.

She didn't want to like him, didn't want to find his smile alluring or his eyes intriguing. He was a Knight, and she needed to remember that. She was about to say goodbye and end the conversation before it really had a chance to start, when the restaurant door opened and her mother and Dan stepped onto the sidewalk.

"Marnie, you're still here?" Helen said.

"Jack, you're here early," Dan said.

The pieces clicked together in Marnie's mind. The timing of Jack's arrival. *Picking up my father,* he'd said.

She glanced from one man to the other, and prayed she was wrong. "Dan's your father?" she said to Jack, then spun back to Dan. "But...but your last name is Simpson."

Dan grinned. "Guilty as charged. I'm this troublemaker's stepfather." He draped a loving arm around Jack and gave him a quick hug.

"You know Dan's son?" Helen asked Marnie. "You never told me that."

"I didn't know until just now. And, Ma, I think you should know that Jack..." Marnie started to tell her mother the rest, the truth about who Jack was, but she watched the light in her mother's eyes dim a bit, and she couldn't do it. The urge to keep the peace, to keep everyone happy, overpowered the words and she let them die in her throat.

Dan Simpson. Father of Jack Knight, the man whose company had ruined her family's life.

Dan Simpson. The man her mother was falling for.

Dan Simpson. Another Mr. Wrong in a family teeming with them.

"You should know that, uh, Jack and I met the other night," Marnie said finally. "We sort of…ran into each other."

"Oh, my. What a small world," Helen said, beaming again.

"Getting smaller every day." Jack grinned at Marnie, but the smile didn't sway her. "How do you know my father?"

She gave a helpless shrug. "It seems I just fixed him up with my mother."

"You've got one talented matchmaker standing here," Dan said, giving Helen's hand a squeeze. "You should see if she can fix you up, too, Jack."

Fix him up? She'd rather die first.

"You're a *matchmaker?*" Jack raised a brow in amusement.

"Guilty as charged," she said, echoing Dan's words.

Her brain swam with the incongruity of the situation. How could she have created such a disaster? Usually her instincts were right on, but this time, they had failed her. And she'd created a mess of epic proportion. One that was slipping out of her control more every second.

Beside her, Dan and Helen were chatting, making plans for dinner or lunch or something. They were off to the side, caught in their own world of just the two of them. All of Marnie's senses were attuned to Jack—the enemy of her family and son of the man who had finally put a smile on her mother's face. How was she supposed to tell Ma the truth, and in the process, break a heart that had just begun to mend?

Jack leaned in then, close, his breath a heated whisper against her ear. "I'm surprised you didn't try to fix me up the night we met."

"I wouldn't do that to one of my clients," she whispered back.

Confusion filled his blue eyes, a confusion she had no intent of erasing, not here, not now.

"I'm not sure what I did to make you despise me," he said, "but I assure you, I'm not nearly as bad as you think."

"No, you're not," she said just as the valet arrived with her car. She opened the door, and held Jack's gaze over the roof. "You're worse."

Then she got in her car and pulled away.

A matchmaker.

Of all the jobs Jack would have thought the fiery redhead Marnie Franklin held, matchmaker sat at the very bottom of the list. Yet, the title seemed to suit her, to match her strong personality, her crimson hair, her quick tongue.

His stepfather had raved about Marnie's skills the entire ride from the restaurant to the repair shop to pick up the car the taxi driver had rear-ended, return the rental, then head home. The event had agreed with Dan, giving his hearty features a new energy, and his voice renewed enthusiasm, as if he'd reverse-aged in one afternoon. At six-foot two, with a full head of gray hair, Dan cut an imposing figure offset by a ready smile and pale green eyes. Eyes that now lit with joy every time he talked about Helen.

"I never would have expected to fall for the matchmaker's mother," Dan said. "But I tell ya, Jack, I really like Helen."

"I'm glad," Jack said. And he was. His stepfather had been alone for a long, long time, and deserved happiness. Just with someone other than Marnie Franklin's maternal relatives. The woman had something against him, that was clear.

"Her daughter's quite pretty, too, you know," Dan said.

"Really? I hadn't noticed."

Dan laughed. "You lie about as well as I cook. I saw you checking her out."

"That was a reflex."

"Sure it was." Dan shifted in his seat to study his son. "You know, you should use some of the arguments you used on me."

Jack concentrated on the road. Boston traffic in the middle of the day required all his attention. Yeah, that was why he didn't look Dan in the eye. Because of the cars on the road. "What are you talking about?"

"The list of reasons why I should go to that event—and I'm glad I did, by the way—is the same list I should give you about why you should ask Marnie out."

"I did. She turned me down."

"And?"

"And what? End of story." He didn't want to get into the reasons why he had no intentions of dating anyone right now. He, of all people, should steer far and wide from anything resembling a relationship.

He could bring a business back to life, turn around a lackluster bottom line, but when it came to personal relationships, he was—

Well, Tanya had called him unavailable. Uninvolved. Cold, even. More addicted to his smartphone than her.

A year after the end of their relationship, he'd had to admit she had a point. When he woke up in the morning, his first thought was the latest business venture, not the woman in his life.

Then why had he asked Marnie to coffee?

Because for the first time in a long time, he was intrigued. She'd been on his mind ever since the night they'd met. Confounding, intriguing Marnie Franklin had been a constant thought in the back of his head. After seeing her today, those thoughts had moved front and center. But he didn't tell Dan any of this, because he knew it would give his stepfather more ammunition for his "get back to dating" argument.

Right now, Jack was concentrating on work, and on making amends. Jack Knight, Sr. had ruined a lot of lives, and Jack had spent the last two years trying to undo the damage his father had done, while still keeping the business going and keeping the people who worked for him employed. As soon as he'd moved into his father's office, he'd vowed he would do things differently, approach the company in a new way. He'd gone through all the old files, and had tried to apply that philosophy, one deal at a time.

Tanya might not have thought he had heart when it came to personal relationships, but Jack was determined to prove the opposite in his business relationships. That uninvolved, cold man he'd been was slowly being erased as he gave back more than Knight had taken.

More than he himself had taken.

To try his best to be everything except his father's son.

That, Jack knew, was why he kept putting in all those hours. He'd been part of his father's selfish, greedy machinations, and it was all Jack could do now to restore what had been destroyed, partly by his own hand.

Doing so felt good, damned good, but he knew the time he invested in that goal was costing him a life, a family, kids. Maybe if he could do enough to make amends to all those his father had wronged, when he went to sleep at night, then maybe the past would stop haunting him.

And then he could look to the future again.

Maybe.

It hadn't thus far, and there were days when he wondered if he was doing the right thing. Or just trying to fill an endless well of guilt.

"What do you want to do for dinner?" Jack said, changing the subject.

"You're on your own tonight, kid. I have plans with Helen." Dan grinned, and for a second, Jack envied his stepfather that beaming smile, that anticipation for the night ahead. "I'm taking her to Top of the Hub."

Jack arched a brow at the mention of the famous moving restaurant at the top of the Prudential building. "Impressive. On a first date?"

"Gotta wow her right off," Dan said.

"I must have missed the memo."

Dan chuckled. "You're just a little jaded right now."

"Not jaded. More…realistic about my strengths. I'm good at business, not good at relationships. End of story."

"Hey, you're preaching to the choir here," Dan said. "I'm the king of bad at relationships, or at least I used to be. You live and you learn, and hopefully stop making the mistakes that screwed up your last relationship."

Which was the one skill Jack had yet to master. When it came to businesses and bottom lines, he could shift gears and learn from the past. But with other people… not so much. Maybe it was because he had gone too many years trying to prove himself to a father who didn't love him or appreciate him. Jack had kept striving for a connection that never existed. That made him either a glutton for punishment or a fool. "Or just avoid relationships all together."

Dan chuckled. "What are you going to do? Become a monk?"

"I don't know. Think they're taking applications?" Jack grinned. Nah, he wouldn't become a monk, but he wasn't at a point in his life where he wanted or needed a committed relationship.

He was trying to buckle down and do the right thing where Knight Enterprises was concerned. Juggling yet another commitment seemed like an impossible task. Deep down inside, he worried more about getting too close to a woman. He'd screwed things up with Tanya, and had plenty of relationship detritus in his past to prove his lack of commitment skills. He had been his father's son in business—and a part of Jack wondered if he'd be his son in a marriage, too. The easiest course—keep his head down and his focus on work. Rather than try to fix the one part of his life that had been impossible to repair.

"When do I have time to date?" Jack said. "I barely have enough spare time to order a pizza."

Except he had found plenty of time to think and wonder about Marnie. His wandering mind had set him a good day behind on his To Do list. He really needed to focus, not daydream. By definition, the sassy matchmaker believed in destiny and true love and all of that. Jack, well, Jack hadn't been good at either of those.

"Aw, you meet Miss Right and you'll change your tune," Dan said. "Like me. Helen has me rethinking this whole love in the later years concept."

"All that from one meeting?"

"I told you, she's a special lady. When you know, you know."

Jack would argue with that point. He'd never had that all-encompassing, couldn't-talk-about-anything-else feeling for a woman before.

Well, that was, until he met Marnie. She'd stuck in his mind like bubble gum, sweet, delicious, addictive. Maybe Dan had a point. But in the end, Jack still sucked at relationships and pursuing Marnie Franklin could only end with a broken heart. But that didn't stop him from wanting her or wondering about her. And why her attitude toward him had done a sudden 180.

Had his reputation preceded him? Had he hurt her somehow, too, in the years he'd worked with his father? Jack decided to do a little research in the morning and see if there was a connection. A memory nagged in the back of his head, but didn't take hold.

Jack pulled in front of the renovated brownstone where he lived, a building much like himself—filled with unique character, a speckled history, but still a little rough around the edges.

While his stepfather headed off—whistling—to the shower, Jack grabbed a bag of chips, taking them out to the balcony. He scrolled through his phone, past the endless stream of emails and voice mails. Work called to him, a non-stop siren of demands. On any other day, he'd welcome the distraction and challenges. But not today. Today, he just wanted to sit back, enjoy the sunshine and think about the choices he'd made.

Maybe his stepfather had a point. Maybe it was time to date again, to make a serious commitment to something other than a cell phone plan and a profit and loss statement. He'd been working for two years to make up for the past, and still it hadn't fulfilled him like he thought it would. Nor had it eased the guilt that haunted his nights. It was as if he was missing something, some key that would bring it all together. Or maybe Dan was right and Jack needed to open his heart, too. A monumental task, and one he had never tackled successfully before.

He took a chip, the fragile snack crumbling in his hand, and thought maybe he was a fool for believing in things that could crumble at any moment.

CHAPTER THREE

As soon as her mother left on her date with Dan that night, the condo echoed. Empty, quiet. Helen had been at Marnie's house for the better part of the afternoon, indulging in a lot of mother-daughter chatting and taking a whirl through Marnie's closet to borrow a fun, flirty dress. Helen's contagious verve had Marnie in stitches, laughing until her sides hurt. But once Ma was gone, the mood deflated and reality intruded.

Marnie tried working, gave up, and gathered her planner and laptop into a big tote and headed out the door. Five minutes later, she was sweating on a treadmill at the gym near her house. It had been weeks since she'd had time for a good workout and as the beats drummed in her head, and the cardio revved up her heart, the stresses of the day began to melt away.

Someone got on the treadmill beside her, but Marnie didn't notice for a few seconds. As she passed the three-mile mark, she pressed the speed button, slowing her pace to a fast walk. Her breath heaved in and out of her chest, but in a good way, giving her that satisfaction of a hard job done well.

"You're making me feel like a couch potato."

She swiveled her head to the right, and saw Jack Knight, doing an easy jog on the other treadmill. Her hand reached up, unconsciously brushing away the sweat on her brow and giving her bangs a quick swipe. Damn. She should have put on some makeup or lip gloss or something. Then she cursed herself for caring how she looked. She wasn't interested in Jack Knight or what he thought about her, all sweaty and messy. Not one bit.

Then why did her gaze linger on his long, defined legs, his broad chest? Why did she notice the way the simple gray T and dark navy shorts he wore gave him a casual, sexy edge? Why did her heart skip a beat when he smiled at her? And why did her hormones keep ignoring the direct orders from her brain?

"I'm impressed." He glanced at the digital display on her treadmill. "Great pace, nice distance."

"Thanks." She took her pace down another notch, and pressed the cool down button. "Are you a member at this gym? I've never seen you here before."

"That's because most of the time, I'm here in the middle of the night, after I finally leave the office for the day. At that time, I have the whole place pretty much to myself."

She gave him a quizzical look. "I thought the gym closes at ten."

"It does. I have...special privileges." He broke into a light jog, arms moving, legs flexing. His effortless run caused a modest uptick in his breathing, leaving Marnie the one now impressed. She'd have been huffing and puffing by now.

"Let me guess," she said. "A cute girl at the front desk gave you a key?"

"Nope. My key comes from one of the owners."

"You?"

"I don't own it," he said. "I have a...vested interest in this gym. One of my high school friends bought it, and when he was struggling, he needed an investor, so I stepped in."

"You did?" She tried to keep the surprise from her voice, but didn't quite make it. "That's really...nice."

Not the kind of thing she expected from Jack Knight, evil corporate raider. He'd saved the gym owned by his friend, but not her father's business. Did he only help friends? And let a stranger's businesses fall to pieces? Or was there a nice guy buried deep inside him?

Or were there a few things she hadn't accepted about her father's company and his role in its demise?

A part of Marnie had always avoided looking too close at the details, because keeping them at bay let her keep her focus on Knight as the evil conglomerate at fault. But deep down inside Marnie knew her affable, distracted, creative father wasn't the best businessman in the world. Helen refused to talk about it, refused to open those "dark doors" as she called them, to the past. And right now, right here, Marnie didn't want to open them either.

Jack leaned over, the scent of soap and man filling the space between them and sending that zing through Marnie all over again. "See? I told you, I'm not as bad as you think I am."

Her face heated. She reached for the hand towel on the treadmill and swiped at her cheeks, then took a deep gulp of water from her water bottle. "I never said you were a horrible person."

Out loud.

"You didn't have to. It was in the way you drove away from the restaurant earlier and in your stinging rejection of my invitation to coffee." He bumped up the speed on his treadmill and increased his jog pace, his arms moving in concert with his legs. "And it was just coffee, Marnie, not a lifetime commitment."

He was right. A cup of coffee with a handsome man wasn't a crime.

Except this handsome man was Jack Knight, who had destroyed her father's company in one of his "investments." She doubted he even realized what he had done to her family, and how that loss had hurt all of them in more than just Tom Franklin's bank account.

She opened her mouth to tell him what she really thought of him, then stopped herself. That urge to keep the peace resurged, coupled with a burst of protectiveness. If Marnie lashed out at Jack, the conversation would get back to Dan and her mother. She had yet to tell her mother who Dan really was, unable to bring herself to wipe that smile off Helen's face, to hurt her mother or disappoint her. Somehow, she had to tell her the truth, though, and do it soon.

Wouldn't it be smart to go into that conversation armed with information? And the best way to gather information without the other party suspecting? Dine with the enemy.

Maybe her father hadn't been businessman of the year, but she knew as well as she knew her own name that Knight Enterprises had been part of the company's downfall, too. If she could figure out how and why, then she could go to her mother and warn her away from Dan. Maybe then both Franklin women would have closure…and peace.

"You know, you're right. It's not a lifetime commitment," she said before she could think twice. "I'll take you up on your coffee offer."

He arched a brow in surprise, and turned toward her, but didn't slow his pace. "Where and when?"

"As soon as you finish your run. If that works for you."

Jack glanced at the time remaining on the treadmill's display and nodded. "Sounds good. How about if I meet you up front in twenty minutes?"

Enough time for her to hit the locker room and get cleaned up. Not that she cared what she looked like with Jack Knight, of course. It was merely because she was going out in public.

As she stepped into the shower and washed up, she second guessed her decision. Getting close to Jack Knight could be dangerous on a dozen different levels. A matchmaker knew better than to put Romeo and Juliet together—and especially not enemies like her and Jack. She had no business seeing him, dating him, or even thinking about either.

She still remembered her father's heartbreak, how he had become a shell of the man he used to be, sitting at home, purposeless, waiting for a miracle that never came. His life's work, gone in an instant. And all because of Jack Knight.

The last of the lather went down the shower drain. She'd have coffee with Jack, and in the process, maybe find a way to exact a little revenge for how he had let her father fail, rather than help the struggling businessman succeed.

What was that they said about revenge? That it was a dish best served cold? Well, this one was going to be rich, dark and steaming hot.

Seventeen minutes later, Jack stood in the lobby of the health club, showered, changed, and his heart beating a mile a minute. He told himself it was from the hard, short run on the treadmill, but he knew better. There was something about Marnie Franklin that intrigued him in ways he hadn't been intrigued in a hell of a long time.

Her smile, for one. It lit her green eyes, danced in her features, seemed to brighten the room.

Her sass, for another. Marnie was a woman who could clearly give as good as she got, and that was something he didn't often find.

Her love/hate for him, for a third. He knew attraction, and could swear she'd been attracted to him when they first met. Then somewhere along the way, she'd started to dislike him. Yet at the same time, she seemed to war with those two emotions.

He had done some preliminary research before he hit the gym, but his files were filled with Franklins, a common enough last name. Then it hit him.

Tom Franklin.

A printer, with a small shop in Boston. Nice guy, but such a muddled, messy businessman that Jack had at first balked when his father asked him to take on Top Notch Printing as a client. He hadn't realized at the time what his father's real plan was—

Well, maybe he had, and hadn't wanted to accept the truth. Buy up the company for pennies on the dollar, to pave the way for a big-dollar competitor moving into town, another branch of the Knight investment tree. Within weeks, Tom Franklin had been out of business.

Oh, damn. If Marnie was that Franklin, Jack had a hell of a lot to make up for. And no idea how to do it. Jack's memory told him that none of Tom's daughters had been named Marnie, though, so he couldn't be sure. Maybe it was all some kind of weird coincidence.

Just then Marnie came down the hall, wearing a navy and white striped skirt that swooshed around her knees, and a bright yellow blouse that offset the deep red of her hair. She had on flats, which was a change from the heels he'd seen her in before, but on Marnie, they looked sweet, cute. Her skin still had that dewy just showered look, and like the other two times he'd seen her, she'd put her hair back in a clip that left a few stray tendrils curling along her neck. The whole effect was… devastating. His fingers itched to see what it would take to get her to let her hair down, literally and figuratively. To see Marnie Franklin unfettered, wild, sexy.

"Where are we going?" she asked. "There's that chain coffee shop—"

He shook his head. "I'm not exactly a decaf venti kind of guy. When I want coffee, I want just that. So, the question is—" at this he took a step closer to her, telling himself it was just to catch a whiff of that intoxicating perfume she wore, a combination of flowers and dark nights "—do you trust me?"

Her eyes widened and she inhaled a quick breath. Then a grin quirked up on one side of her face, and she raised her chin a notch. Sassy. "No, I don't. But I'll take my chances anyway."

"Pretty risky."

"I'm not worried. I carry pepper spray."

A laugh burst out of him, then he turned and opened the health club door for her. As she ducked past him, he leaned in again and caught another whiff of that amazing perfume. Damn sexy, and addictive. "You surprise me, Marnie Franklin. Not too many people do that."

"I'll keep that in mind." She tossed the last over her shoulder, before walking into the waning sunshine.

He fell into step beside her, the two of them shifting into small talk about the weather and the treadmills at the gym as they walked down the busy main street for a couple of blocks before turning right on a small side street. Dusk had settled on the city. Coupled with the dark overlay of leafy trees it made for a cozy, peaceful stroll. For Jack, the walk was as familiar as the back of his hand.

He knew he should find a way to bring the conversation around to whether her father was the Tom Franklin he'd known, but Jack couldn't do it. He liked Marnie, liked her a lot. If she had a chance to get to know this Jack, the one who had walked away from his father's legacy and now tried to do things differently, then maybe he could explain what had happened before.

"Where are we going?" Marnie asked.

"It's a surprise. You'll see."

"Okay, but I don't have a ton of time—"

He put a hand on her arm, a quick, light touch, but it seemed to sear his skin, and he saw her do another quick inhale and a part of him—the part that had been closed off for so long—came to life. He wanted to let her in, if only for today, to have a taste of that sweet lightness, even though he feared a woman like her wasn't meant for a man like him.

"It's beautiful out. We both work hard. I think we can afford a few extra minutes to enjoy the end of the day."

She gave him a wary glance. "Okay. But just a few."

The side street led straight into a neighborhood, as if stepping into another world after leaving the hecticness of the city. Quiet descended over the area, while the constant hum of rush hour traffic behind them got farther away with each step. Elegant brick homes nearly as old as Boston itself decorated either side of the street, fronted by planters filled with bright, happy flowers. Concrete sidewalks lined either side of the street, accented with grassy strips and the minutiae of life in a neighborhood—kids' bikes, lawn tools, newspapers. Neighbors greeted Jack as he walked by, and passing cars slowed to give him a wave.

In the distance, the gold-tipped spire of a church peeked above the leafy green trees, like a crown on top of a perfect cake. His heart swelled the farther he walked. No matter how many times he came back here, he always felt the same—at home.

"How come everyone knows you here?" Marnie said.

"I grew up in this neighborhood, staying in the same house all my life, even after my mom married Dan," he said. "Even though my dad passed away and my mom moved to Florida a couple years ago, this place is still home."

"It's a pretty neighborhood. Lots of great architecture." She raised a hand to touch the black curved iron and aluminum pole of the street light. It was a replica, and a pretty darn close historical copy of the original lights that had been lit by torches a century ago. "I love these lights, too. The old-fashioned ones are my favorite."

"Much nicer than the sodium vapor and high mast ones they use on the main roads. And in keeping with the tradition that's so important to this neighborhood."

"Oh, and look, daisies." She pointed to a house fronted by the bright white flowers. "I loved those when I was a kid, so much that my dad called me Daisy-doo. Silly, but you know, when it's your dad, it's kinda special."

"I bet." His father had never been the kind for anything as superfluous as a nickname. Dan had been the one to tease, make jokes, envelop Jack with warmth and hugs. But the man whose DNA Jack shared, hadn't done so much as offer a hug.

He shrugged off the memories and pointed to the spire. "Back when this neighborhood was built, it was centered around the church. It's still pretty central to the houses here."

They rounded another corner, and as they did, the road opened up, showcasing a simple white building. The small, unpretentious church sat in the middle of the neighborhood, with the rest of the streets jutting off like spokes. Street lights blinked to life, and danced golden light over the sidewalk. "This is my favorite time of day to be here," Jack said. "It looks so beautiful and peaceful. So pristine and perfect, like a new beginning could be had for the asking."

He hadn't realized he'd said that out loud until Marnie turned to him and smiled. "That sounds so… awesome."

"Thanks. But I can't take all the credit." He gestured toward the building.

Marnie stopped walking and stared up at the church. "Wow. It *is* beautiful. Understated. Maybe because it's so…ordinary. There are so many buildings in this city that try to compete for architectural design of the year, and this one is more…wholesome, if that makes sense."

"It does. I guess that's why I like coming here."

"You go to this church?"

He nodded. "I've gone almost every Sunday since the day I was born."

She arched a brow. "Really? You?"

He leaned in again, close enough to see the flecks of gold in her eyes, the soft chestnut wave brushing against her cheek. And close enough to once again, be mesmerized by her perfume. "I told you, I'm not as bad as you think."

She raised her gaze to his, and that smile returned. "You don't know what I think about you, Mr. Knight."

He reached up and trailed a finger down her cheek, whisking away that errant hair before lowering his hand. She inhaled, exhaled, watching him. No, he didn't know what she thought about him. But damn, he wanted to know.

Was it just because she was trying so hard not to like him? Or because he was tired of being seen as the evil corporate raider, painted with the same brush as his father?

Jack just wanted time before he probed deeper, to find out where Marnie's animosity lay. Give her a chance to get to know this Jack Knight, the one who no longer did his father's bidding. Then, when the time was right, he'd broach the subject of the past. Because right now he wanted her. Damn, did he want her.

"Considering how much we have in common, Marnie," he said, "I think you should call me by my first name. Don't you?"

"And what do we have in common?"

"Besides an appreciation for good architecture, and a competitive streak on the treadmill, there's the fact that our parents are dating."

She laughed. "In my world, that's not something in common. Heck, that wouldn't even be enough to invite you to a mixer, *Mr. Knight.*"

Damn. Every time he thought they were growing closer, that she was giving him a chance, she retreated, threw up a wall. They started walking again, circling past the church, then turning down another tree-lined street. They walked at an easy pace, no hurry to their step. How long had it been since he'd done that? Taken a walk, with no real hurry to his journey? Even though he had a thousand things to do, at least a dozen phone calls to return and countless emails waiting for his attention, he kept walking. Something about today, or about Marnie, made him want to linger rather than rush back to the office. Right now, he couldn't tell if that was a good or bad thing.

"So how does it work?" he asked.

They passed under a leafy maple tree, the branches hanging so low, they whispered across their heads. "What? Matchmaking?" she said.

He nodded. "Do you use some kind of algorithm or something? A computer program?"

"No." She laughed. "Most of it's instinct. We do log pertinent client and potential match information into the computer, just so it's easier to develop a list of bachelors or bachelorettes for a mixer, but when it comes to picking the best possible matches, it's all in here." She pressed a hand to her chest.

He jerked his gaze up and away from the enticing swell of her breast. He was having a conversation here, not indulging in a fantasy. Except every time he looked at her, his thoughts derailed. Especially when she smiled like she did, or laughed that lyrical laugh of hers. "Sounds sort of like buying a business. Instinctually, I know which ones will be the best choice, and which aren't going to make it, no matter how much of a cash infusion I give it."

Her expression hardened. "Yeah, I bet it's exactly like that. All guts. No logic." She cast her glance to the right and left, away from him. The warm and bubbly moments between them evaporated, and a wall of ice dropped into her voice. "So, where's this coffee shop?"

Her reaction sealed his suspicions. She'd been

burned, either by Knight or someone like him. But most likely his company. Guilt churned in his stomach.

"One more block," he said, trying to redirect the conversation. "Close enough to walk there after church, which is part of what makes the location so ideal."

The wall remained, however. Silence descended on them, an uncomfortable, tense hole in the conversation. They reached the corner where the coffee shop sat, a bright burst amidst the brick and white of the neighborhood.

The door to the Java Depot was propped open, and the rich scent of brewed coffee wafted outside, luring customers in with its siren call of caffeine. Several couples sat at umbrella-covered wrought iron tables, while a trio of kids played on the small playground set up beside the shop's deck. The non-lucrative use of a good chunk of the cafe's land had been a risky move, but one that had paid off, given the number of kids and families that visited this space on a regular basis. The sound system played contemporary jazz and alternative music, lots of it by local artists who often performed on the outdoor patio.

"Cute place," Marnie said. "I never even knew it existed."

"One of those great hidden secrets in Boston." He grinned. "Though the new owner is determined to get the word out via advertising and social media."

Marnie looked around, her intelligent gaze assessing the location and décor. "I like how it's so community oriented, with the local art displays, and the playground for kids. It's almost like being at home."

The words warmed him. He so rarely saw the reaction to his work, the money he invested, the counsel he gave. Too often, he'd seen the effects of the businessman he used to be—the shuttered shops, the For Sale signs, the people filing unemployment. But the Java Depot was a success story, one of many, he hoped. Appreciation and seeing others' success was a far greater reward than any increase in his own bottom line.

"That was the idea. A neighborhood coffee shop should feel like an ingrained part of the neighborhood and reflect the owner's personality. This one does both." He waved her ahead of him, then stepped inside and paused while his eyes adjusted to the dim interior.

"Jack!" Dorothy, a platinum blond buxom woman in her fifties who had been behind the counter of the Java Depot for nearly two years, sent him a wave. She gave him a broad, friendly smile, as if she was greeting a long lost family member. Considering how long he'd known Dot, she practically was family. "I brewed some of your favorite blend today. Let me get you a cup."

"Thanks, Dot. And I'll need a…" He glanced at Marnie.

"Whatever you're having. But with the girly touch of some cream and sugar."

"A second one. Regular, please."

"You got it," Dot said. A few seconds later, she passed two steaming mugs of coffee across the counter. "Got fresh baked peanut butter cookies, too." Before he could respond, she laid two cookies on a plate and slid those over, too, giving Jack a wink.

"You are bad for my diet, Dot." He grinned.

"You work it off in smiles, you charmer, you." She chuckled, then turned to Marnie. "Half my waitstaff trips over themselves to serve him. There's going to be a lot of envious eyes on you, my girl, because you've snagged Mr. Eligible here."

"Oh, I'm not his girlfriend," Marnie said. Fast. So fast, a man could take it personally.

"Well, you're missing out on a hell of a catch," Dot said, then gave Jack a wink. "Why this man is the whole reason I'm in business. Without Jack, there wouldn't be a Java Depot here. He helped me out, encouraged me, gave me great advice, and a big old nudge when I needed one most. Always has, and I suspect even if I tell him not to, he always will." Dot's light blue eyes softened when she looked over at Jack. "It's good to have you in my corner, Jack."

He shifted his weight, uncomfortable under Dot's grateful words. It was what he worked for, but there were days when praise for doing the right thing felt like wearing the wrong shoes. Maybe someday he'd get used to it.

"I needed a place to get my coffee," he said. "And my mom is addicted to your cookies, so if you went out of business and stopped shipping them down to her in Florida, she'd go into serious withdrawal, and I'd have hell to pay."

"Yeah, that's why you helped me out," Dot said with a little snort of disbelief. "Purely selfish reasons."

Jack grinned and put up his hands. "That's me."

Dot shook her head, then gestured toward Marnie. "He's a keeper, I'm telling you. Though you might have to beat off half the women in Boston to get him. And you—" she wagged a finger at Jack "—you need to use some of that legendary Knight charm, and win her over." Dot chuckled, then headed to the other end of the counter to help another customer.

"Legendary charm?" Marnie asked. She reached past him to pick up her mug of coffee, and give him a teasing grin. "Legendary like the Loch Ness Monster and Bigfoot?"

"Exactly." He chuckled, then picked up the second mug and the cookies and followed her to an outdoor table where Christmas lights lit the undersides of the umbrellas over the tables. A soft breeze rippled the bright blue umbrella, and toyed with the ends of Marnie's hair. His fingers ached to do the same.

He'd thought he didn't want to date anyone. That he didn't have room in his life for a relationship. A week ago, he would have sworn up and down that he had no interest in dating anyone on a long-term basis. That he, of all people, shouldn't try to create ties.

Then he met Marnie.

Maybe it was the way she ran hot, then cold. Maybe it was the way she kept him at a distance, like a book he couldn't read in the library. Or maybe it was that none of his "legendary charm" worked on her. Was it about the challenge of wanting what he couldn't have? Or something more?

Either way, he reminded himself, he was his father's son. The offspring of a womanizer who destroyed companies, ruined lives, and broke hearts. Jack had been like that, too, for too long. He'd managed to change his approach to business, but when it came down to making a commitment, would he run like his father had or stick around? Would he shut out the people he cared for, turn his back on them?

Marnie picked up one of the cookies, and took a bite. A smattering of crumbs lingered on her lips, and it took everything in his power not to kiss her. Then the family beside them got up and left, leaving him and Marnie alone on the patio. She reached for her coffee, and before he could think twice, he leaned forward, closing the distance between them to mere inches. Desire thundered in his veins, pounded in his brain. All he wanted right now was her, that sweet goodness, her tempting smile. To hell with later; Jack wanted now. "You have a crumb right—"

And he kissed her. To hell with staying away, to hell with making smart decisions, to hell with everything but this moment.

A gentle kiss, more of a whisper against her lips. She froze for a second, then shifted closer to him, one hand reaching to cup his cheek, her fingers dancing against his skin. She deepened the kiss, her delicate tongue slipping in to tango with his. Holy cow. A hot, insistent need ignited in his veins, and it took near every ounce of his strength to pull back instead of taking her on the table in front of the whole damned neighborhood.

"Uh, I think I got it," he said. Truth was, right now he couldn't think or see straight enough to tell if she was covered in crumbs.

Her fingers went to her mouth, lingered a moment, then she lowered her hand. Her cheeks flushed a deep pink and she let out a soft curse. "That...that wasn't a good idea. At all. I have to go." She got to her feet, leaving the half-eaten cookie on the plate. "Thanks for the coffee."

"Wait, Marnie—"

"Jack, stay out of my life. You've done enough damage already."

Then she turned and left. Jack leaned back in his chair and watched her go, bemused and befuddled. A woman who kissed him back yet claimed not to be interested in him. She was a puzzle, that was for sure. What had she meant by "you've done enough damage already"?

A sinking feeling told him she'd meant more than that kiss. His past had reared its ugly head again. Somewhere, Marnie was connected to the mistakes he'd made years before. He vowed to dig deeper into the files in his office, and find the connection.

Would it always be this way? Would he find his regrets confronting him every time he tried to do the right thing?

Jack watched Marnie hail a cab, get inside the yellow taxi and disappear into the congested streets. Somehow, he needed to find a way to do what he had done before. Mitigate the damage. And find a solution that left everyone happy.

CHAPTER FOUR

JACK LOGGED A hard six miles on the treadmill, but it wasn't enough. He could have run a marathon and it wouldn't have been enough to quiet the demons in his head. He'd tried, Lord knew he'd tried, over the years.

By the time he climbed off the machine, he was drenched in sweat, but his mind still raced with thoughts of Marnie Franklin. Hell, half the reason he'd come to the gym today was because he'd hoped to bump into her.

After their walk to the coffee shop, he'd gone to the office and pulled out Top Notch Printing's file, from the piles stacked on the credenza behind his desk. So many people's lives ruined, so many businesses shuttered, their contents sold like trinkets at a garage sale.

He'd dug through Tom's file, looking for the notes he'd made all those years ago.

Owner: Tom Franklin, married to wife Helen. Three daughters. Calls them Daisy, Kitty and Chatterbug.

Nicknames. That's why Jack hadn't made the connection when he'd met Marnie. He'd never known Tom's daughters' real names, never spent enough time with the man to get that personal.

Jack dropped onto a bench outside the gym and put his head in his hands. He could still see Tom's face. Bright, hopeful, trusting. Believing every word Jack and his father said.

Jack had tried to undo the damage, but by then it had been too late. Too damned late.

He sighed and got to his feet. Instead of taking the left toward the office, he took a right and went back home.

"I thought you just left. What are you doing home so soon?" his stepfather asked when Jack stepped into the apartment.

"I'm off to a slow start today." Because his mind was far from work. Had been ever since Marnie's cab had dented his sports car. That alone was a sign he was in too deep. Then why kiss her? Why go to the gym on the off chance she'd be there, too? Why couldn't he just forget her? Was it all about trying to make up for the past? Or more?

"Maybe I need some protein or something. You want to go grab some breakfast before I head into the office? Unless you already ate."

"Even if I did, I'll eat again." Dan chuckled, and grabbed a light jacket off the back of the kitchen chair. "That's the beauty of retirement. No schedule. Lunch can come five minutes after breakfast."

They headed out into the bright sunshine and around the corner to Hector's cozy little deli. Its glass windows looked out onto two streets, while inside, business bustled along, in keeping with the city's busy pace. Hector greeted them as they walked in with a boisterous hello and a hearty wave. A gregarious guy given to playing mariachi music just because, Hector was a colorful and exuberant addition to the area. His incredible sandwiches drew people far and wide for their unique taste combinations and home-baked breads.

Dan and Jack ordered, then snagged a couple of bar stools at the window counter, and unwrapped their sandwiches. "So, what do you think of Helen?" Dan asked.

Dan and Helen had been on several dates over the last week. Dan had even invited her to dinner at Jack's apartment—and wisely ordered takeout instead of trying to cook. They'd gone to a Red Sox game, played Bingo at a local church and taken several long walks through the neighborhood. After every date, Dan's smile grew broader, his step lighter, like a man falling in love.

"She seems really nice," Jack said. "And she definitely likes you."

A big, goofy grin spread over Dan's face. "I sure like her, too. More and more every day." Dan toyed with the paper wrapper before him. "You're okay with me dating? I mean, it's got to be kind of weird."

"You and my mom divorced years ago, Dad." Even though Dan was his stepfather, he'd been in Jack's life for so long, calling him Dad seemed natural. Jack's real father had left him the business, and not much else, letting his work keep him from seeing his son, and leaving the raising of Jack up to Dan and Helen. Probably for the best, because Dan had been a hell of a stepfather. Jack, Senior had been about as warm and fuzzy as a porcupine.

Still, there'd always been that part of Jack that had craved a relationship with his biological father. Maybe because then he could have the answers he wanted about why Jack, Sr. had walked away from his family. Why he had chosen work over his son. In the end, Jack had realized his father lacked the capacity to love others first.

And that he had been damned lucky to have Dan, who had shown him the way a good father acted.

"I want you to be happy, too," Jack said to Dan, and meant the words.

"Me, too. And hopefully, I do it right this time."

"About doing things right…" Jack sighed. "There's something you should know. Helen is the widow of one of the business owners that Knight put out of business."

"She mentioned something about her husband's company going under after some investors stepped in. I wondered about the connection."

Jack toyed with the napkin. "I was the one that talked Tom into signing with Knight. At the time I was working for my dad and—"

Dan put a hand on his shoulder. "You don't need to explain. We all make mistakes, Jack. We all screw up. The point is you learned and you changed. You're not that man anymore."

Jack nodded, as if he agreed. But he wondered how much distance he had placed between himself and the father he'd idolized. He'd tried so hard to be like him, to get past the wall between them. Had it been at the expense of his heart?

"Why did you and my mom get divorced?" It was a question Jack had never asked. Maybe because he'd been too busy working when the announcement came. Maybe because it was easier to bury himself in work than to call his mom or Dan and ask what had happened. Yet another item to add to his "not good at" list. Family relationships.

Tanya was right. He was cold and uninvolved. He'd cut off the relationships part of his life for far too long. He needed to find more ways to connect, to care. Because if he didn't, he could see the writing on the wall—Jack, Jr., was going to morph into Jack, Sr.

He'd come so close to doing exactly that. Then one day he'd looked in the mirror before the biggest deal of Knight's history, and realized he had become his father, from the mannerisms to the crimson power tie. Jack had walked out of the bathroom, quit his job and walked away.

Dan sighed. "As easy as it would be for me to blame Sarah, truth is, I was a terrible husband."

"You were a great stepdad, though." There'd been after-school softball games in the yard, impromptu weekend camping trips and annual father-son vacations. Dan had gone to every track meet, every Boy Scout canoe trip, every award ceremony.

"Thanks, Jack. You weren't so bad as a stepson yourself." Dan grinned. "But your mother and I, we just didn't have what it took. When we got married, it was a fast decision. Too fast, some would say. We married a week after we met. Crazy, but gosh, I just didn't think it through. I just said I do. By the time I realized we were like oil and water together, it was too late. I'd already started considering you my son, and I couldn't bear leaving. We tried to stick it out after you grew up, but by that time, we'd become two different people, living separate lives. If I had plugged in more, or tried harder, maybe we wouldn't have ended up that way." He sighed. "It was like our marriage died a long, slow death. We were always friends—and we still are—but that wasn't enough to make it work."

Jack had noticed years ago that his mother and Dan rarely hugged or kissed or went out alone. There'd been no drama, no fights, just a quiet existence. Jack couldn't think of anything more agonizing and painful than that.

If he ever settled down, he wanted a woman who challenged him, who made his life an adventure.

A woman like Marnie?

Want if he ended up repeating his father's mistakes? Leaving his wife for one woman after another, ignoring his child, in favor of his company? There was no guarantee Jack would end up doing that, or end up a good man like Dan, but Jack's cautious and logical side threw up a red caution flag all the same.

"I'm glad your mother is happy now with that new guy she's dating," Dan said, bringing Jack back to their conversation. "What's his name? Ray? Seems like he's perfect for her."

Jack had only met Ray once, but he'd have to agree. His mother's new boyfriend was an outgoing, friendly guy who enjoyed the same things as she did—traveling, bike riding, and charitable work. "She needed someone busier than her," Jack said with a chuckle.

Jack's exuberant, spontaneous stepfather had driven his mom crazy sometimes. She was a stick-to-the-schedule, organized woman who never got used to Dan's unconventional approaches. Jack liked to think he'd taken on the best of both their traits. Some of the impulsivity of his stepfather, and some of the dependable keel of his mother. Ray's personality was much closer to Sarah's, which had made them a good fit.

"This time, I'm going to work damned hard to make sure me and the woman I marry are on the same path," Dan said. "And that I let her know all the time how much I appreciate her. Life's too damned short to spend it alone, you know?"

Jack nodded. He'd been feeling the same way himself lately. Was it just because he'd met Marnie? Because he was tired of being alone? Or because he'd glimpsed his future and didn't like the picture it presented? Workaholic, glued to his desk. A repeat of his namesake's choices. Not the future Jack wanted. "You deserve happiness, Dad. You really do."

"Thanks, Jack. That means a lot." Dan took a bite of his sandwich, swallowed, then looked at Jack and a teasing smile lit his face. "How are things going with the daughter?"

"You mean Marnie?" Jack said the word like he didn't know who Dan meant. Like he hadn't been thinking about Marnie almost non-stop for days.

"She's smart and beautiful, and a hell of a catch, according to her mother. And yes, we have been talking about you two and conspiring behind your backs. We both think you'd be a fool to let her get away."

Get away? He couldn't seem to get her to stay. "She's made it very clear that she's not interested in me."

Well, not exactly crystal clear. There was the matter of that kiss. Mixed messages, times ten.

"I think Marnie's figured out my connection to her father's business. It's no wonder she hates me. Seriously, I hate myself for some of the decisions I made back then."

Dan waved that off. "So? You make better decisions now. That's what counts. We're all allowed a little stupidity."

Jack grinned. "Either way, I won't blame Marnie if she wants to tie me to a stake and light a fire at my feet."

"Since when have you let a little roadblock like that hold you back?" Dan chuckled. "Listen, I saw the truth all over her face outside the restaurant the other day. She *likes* you."

Jack snorted.

Dan leaned an arm over his chair. "You know, there is a way to make her prove it."

"What? A little Sodium Pentothal?"

Dan chuckled then leaned in and lowered his voice. "Have her take you on as a client. When she tries to fix you up, she'll see that the best possible match is…"

"Her." Jack let that thought turn around in his head for a while. "It could work. But, I don't know, Dad. I haven't exactly done a good job of balancing work and a life thus far. There's only twenty-four hours in a day and it seems like twenty-three of them are dedicated to the business."

Well, maybe less than that, if he counted the hours spent walking around Boston with Marnie, then at the gym trying to stop thinking about Marnie, and this morning, avoiding the office because all he could do was think about Marnie.

Distracted had become his middle name. Not a good thing right now. He had three pending deals this month, a few other recently acquired companies that still needed his guiding hand, and a To Do list a mile long. And yet, here he was, sitting with Dan and talking about Marnie. He made no move to leave.

Nor did he answer the nagging doubts in his head. The ones that said all he was doing was making excuses. Because that was easier than getting involved—and being the kind of human iceberg that had ruined relationships before.

"Chicken," Dan teased.

"I'm not chicken. I'm busy. There's a difference."

"Bawk, bawk," Dan said, flapping his arms in emphasis. "You are, too. It's time you had a life, Jack, instead of just watching from the sidelines."

He bristled. He'd had the same thoughts, but wouldn't admit it. "I do have a life. I go out, I go to the gym—"

"You *exist.* That's different." Dan clapped a hand on his shoulder, and his light blue eyes met Jack's square-on. "You deserve to be happy. Your father…well, I don't like to speak ill of the dead, but your father wasn't exactly citizen of the year. But that doesn't mean you'll turn out like him. Don't let one bad apple spoil the rest of the batch."

Jack chuckled. "How many trite phrases do you have in you?"

"As many as it takes to get you over to Marnie's office, and back out into the dating world. Who knows, maybe she'll find your perfect match for you."

"I thought the goal was for her to realize she was the right one for me."

"I'm thinking it might need to work both ways," Dan said. "Now get out of here and go over there before you *chicken* out."

"Very funny," Jack said. He got to his feet and tossed his trash in the bin, then said goodbye to his stepfather and left the deli. He stood on the corner for a long moment. To the north lay the office and a thousand responsibilities. To the east, Marnie and a thousand risks.

"What has you all distracted today?" Erica, Marnie's little sister, said. She was sitting at the desk across from Marnie, while the two of them worked on a menu for the annual client thank-you party. Erica had inherited their father's dark brown locks, but the same green eyes as the other Franklin girls. Two years younger than Marnie, she was the bubbly one in the family, filled with more energy than anyone Marnie had ever met.

"Me? I'm not distracted."

Erica laughed. "Uh-huh. Then why did you write the same thing three times on this list? Do we really need that many napkins?" She pointed to a paper sitting between them. "And you've been staring off into space for the last ten minutes. Heck, most of the day I've had to repeat myself every time I've talked to you. This is totally not like you, oh, organized one."

"Sorry. It's just been a busy day." A lie. She had been distracted by thoughts of Jack Knight. What was it about that man? He was the enemy. A man she had done a good job of despising for years.

When she went for coffee with him yesterday, it had been to gather information and come up with a plan for a little revenge. Instead, he'd turned the tables with that kiss.

And what a kiss it had been. As far as kisses went, that one ranked high on Marnie's Top Ten list. She'd gone home after the coffee, and spent half the day doing what she was doing now—daydreaming and wondering how she could be so attracted to a man yet despise him at the same time. Maybe it was some kind of reverse psychology at work.

Or maybe it was that Jack Knight could kiss like no man she'd ever met, and just the mere thought of him sent a delicious rush through her.

God, she was a mess. She needed to get back on track, not keep letting Jack derail her. If there was one thing Marnie excelled at, it was holding on to the reins. She had her business and her apartment organized to the nth degree, her planner filled with neat little squares. She made quarterly goal lists, daily agendas, and didn't go off on crazy heat-filled dates with Mr. Wrong.

Most of the time, anyway.

Then why had she kissed Jack back? Why had she

let him get close? All the more reason to get a grip and get back to work.

The door opened and a burst of yellow rushed into the room. "Oh. My. God. You guys are the *best!*" a female voice screeched.

"Oh, no," Erica whispered and rolled her eyes. Marnie sucked in a fortifying breath.

Every time she arrived, Roberta Stewart's giant personality exploded. A tall, gangly woman, Roberta's decibel-stretching voice entered a room long before she did. Marnie had known her since the first day she opened her doors, one of her first clients—and one of her least successful. Roberta was likeable, smart, and funny, but few people dated her long enough to realize that, because her first impression was so loud and busy. No matter how many times Marnie tried to counsel Roberta to tone it down just a bit, she didn't listen. And the men ran—until they were out of earshot.

Today, Roberta had on a sunny yellow dress that swirled like a bell around her hips, and a wide-brimmed matching hat trimmed with silk orchids. She let out a dramatic sigh, then plopped onto the sofa in the waiting area, her dress spreading across the brown leather like melting butter. "I just came from my *third* engagement party of the year! You guys did it *again!*" Roberta shook her head. "Amy and Bob looked *so happy!*"

"I'm glad," Marnie said, thinking of the cycling enthusiast couple she had put together a few months ago. "They're a great match."

"And now it's my turn!" Roberta jumped to her feet and clasped her hands together. "So, who do you have for me this week? Tell me, who's my new Mr. Right?"

"Things didn't work out with Alan?" Marnie had

really hoped the bookish accountant would be a great counterbalance to Roberta's exuberance.

"Alan, shmalan." Roberta waved a hand in dismissal. "I need a man with verve! Life! Energy! Strength! Somebody's got to keep up with all this!" She swiveled her hips. "And poor Alan was ready to pass out before we even reached the second nightclub. Give me a man who takes his *vitamins!*"

"Maybe you should try a quiet dinner for your first date," Erica said. "Rather than all-night salsa dancing."

"But these shoes and this body were made for *dancing,*" Roberta said. "I need a man who can keep up with me. Call me as soon as you have another one. Oh, and please make sure he's had a stress test before the date. I was a little worried poor Alan's heart was going to go *kaput!*" She gave them a wave, then headed back out the door.

"Ah, Roberta. Always a memorable visit," Erica said once the door shut. "Who are you going to match her with now?"

"I have no idea. I like Roberta, but she needs a very special man." One that had yet to come along, though not for a lack of trying on Marnie's part. Maybe such a bachelor didn't exist in Boston. Or the greater New England area. Or maybe even on planet Earth.

No, there was someone perfect for Roberta. Marnie just hadn't found him yet. He needed to be a unique man, strong yet confident enough to be with a woman like her.

"Speaking of men," Erica said, "I have a date. Mind if I knock off early?"

"Nope. There are no appointments the rest of the day. I'm just going to finish up this menu, and then head home myself."

"Be sure you do," Erica said softly, laying a hand on her sister's shoulder. "Take a little time to let go and just be, sis. Okay?"

"I do."

Erica laughed. "No, you don't. But maybe if I tell you to do it often enough, you finally will."

CHAPTER FIVE

AFTER ERICA LEFT, Marnie sat in her office, the music cranked up on the mini sound system beside her desk, and hammered out the rest of the details for the next few Matchmaking by Marnie events. She spun around in her chair, facing the window that looked out over Brookline, tapping her feet against the sill in time to a catchy pop tune. She'd kicked off her shoes, and let her hair out of the clip that held it in its usual bun. She grabbed a half-eaten bag of chips and started snacking while she watched the traffic go by, singing along between bites, and enjoying her moment of solitude.

"So this is how a matchmaker works her magic."

Marnie gasped, dropped her feet to the floor and spun around, a chip halfway to her mouth, while several more tumbled onto her lap. She wanted to crawl under her desk and hide, or at least shrivel into a bowl. She told herself she didn't care that her hair was a mess, she was covered in potato chip crumbs, and she'd been caught signing off-key to a teenybopper hit.

"Jack…uh, I mean, Mr. Knight," she said, then covered her mouth and paused to swallow. Did she really think calling him by his last name would erase that kiss, the way he made her feel with a simple smile? That it would put up a wall he couldn't pass? She forced authority into her tone. "What are you doing here?"

Even in a dark gray suit, with his pale blue tie loosened at the neck, he looked sexy, approachable. Hard to resist. "I'm looking for a matchmaker," he said. "And you come highly recommended by a close family member. Apparently my stepfather has fallen head over heels for your mother."

"I've heard all about it, too." There was no denying the happiness in Helen's voice. Marnie had talked to her mother earlier today and heard nothing but joy. Hearing that Helen's feelings were reciprocated—

Well, that was what Marnie worked for. The cherry on top of all the work she put in, building that matchmaker sundae. Except her mother was falling for a man with ties to someone who could hurt their family all over again.

"I don't think you need my help," she said. "What was it Dot said? You've got legendary charm? I'm sure you could find plenty of women on your own."

"Whether I do or not, that hasn't brought me Miss Right yet. I think I need a professional." He came closer, then around her desk, to sit on the edge. He leaned forward, and captured a chip just as it began to tumble off her chest. Her face heated. "Someone who knows what they're doing."

She pushed the chair back, and turned to dump the rest of the chips into the trash. That was the last time she was going to eat a messy snack at her desk. "Well, I'm sorry, but I'm not taking new clients right now." A lie. She rarely turned down new clients. In her business, people came and went as their lives changed, which kept her busy year-round and left room for more. "You'll have to find another matchmaker, or maybe try one of those online dating services. Sorry I couldn't help you."

There. That had been definitive, strong. Leaving no room for negotiation—or anything else. But Jack didn't leave. Instead, he leaned in closer, his gaze assessing and probing.

"Okay, tell me." The sun shone through the window and danced gold lights on his hair, his face. "What did I do to you that makes you hate me? Yet, kiss me five minutes later?"

"For your information, that kiss was an accident. I was reacting on instinct."

Why didn't she just tell him the truth? Why did she keep hesitating, letting this flirtatious game continue?

Because a part of her wondered about the man who had helped the local coffee shop and the neighborhood gym and still knew his old neighbors. A part of her wanted to know who the real Jack Knight was.

And if there was a possibility that for all these years, she might have been wrong about him.

"An instinct?" he said, his voice low, dark. "No more?"

"Yes. No more." The lie escaped her in a rush.

"So if I leaned in now—" and he did just that, coming within a whisper of her lips, then brushing his against hers slow, easy, a feather-light kiss that made her want more, before he drew back "—you wouldn't react the same way?"

"Of course not." She stood her ground, but the temptation to curve into him pounded in her veins. To finish what they'd started back in the parking lot, to let that heady, heated rush run through her again, obliterating thought, reason.

Damn it. She didn't do this. She didn't lose control

of her emotions, get swept away by a nice smile and a shimmer of sexual energy. Stupid decisions were made that way, and Marnie refused to do that.

She clenched her fists, released them, and forced her breathing to stay normal, not to betray an ounce of the riot inside her. To not let him know how much she wanted a real, soul-sucking, hot-as-heck kiss right now. Her gaze locked on his, then dropped to his mouth. *Oh, my.*

"Well, I'm glad to know you can resist that 'legendary charm,'" Jack said, then rose and went around her desk to sit in one of the visitor's chairs.

Disappointment whooshed through her. She let out a little laugh to cover the emotion, then sat back in her chair, because her legs had gone to jelly and her heart wouldn't slow. She had two choices right now. Keep denying she was attracted to him, or fix him up and get him out of her life for good. What did she care if he dated half the female population of Boston?

For a woman who craved calm and order more than chips, erasing Jack Knight from her life was the easiest and best option. No one got hurt. A win-win.

"I might be able to help you find someone," she said, clasping her hands on the desk, tight. Treat him like any other client. Act like he's simply another bachelor. "Let's start with why you think this is the right time in your life to find the perfect match?"

He leaned back, propping one leg atop the other. "I think it's time I settled down and pursued the American dream."

"Really? Right now. That's actually what you think." It wasn't a question. Jack coming to her, now, after she'd refused to get close to him, couldn't be a coincidence. It had to be some kind of game. What did he really want?

"It's true. I woke up, realized all my friends are married, have kids, houses in the suburbs. I'm the lone holdout. I guess I haven't met the right woman yet." He grinned.

She let out a gust. "Why are you really here? Because if it's to get me to go out with you, that's not going to work."

"Oh, I know. I got that message. Loud and clear."

She thought she detected a measure of hurt in his voice. Impossible. Jack Knight was a shark, and sharks didn't get hurt feelings. "Well, good."

"My stepfather was very pleased with how compatible he is with Helen, and I thought you could do the same for me."

If Marnie had anything to say about it, her mother would find someone else and stay far, far away from any relative of Jack Knight's. She had yet to find a way to make him pay for the hurt he'd brought to her family.

Confronting him and demanding answers would only backfire when Helen found out. In Marnie's perfect world, Jack Knight was destroyed and her mother never got hurt.

Marnie hadn't been able to keep her mother from being hurt after the death of Tom, but maybe she could make sure this debacle with Jack didn't impact Helen. All she had to do was find a way to keep Jack far from Helen—and that meant making sure Jack got the message that Marnie wanted him gone. She glanced over at the pile on her desk and realized there might be a way to hurt Jack and get rid of him for good—a much better and smarter way than having coffee with him and taking long walks through Boston neighborhoods. Clearly, that kind of thing distracted her too much. Brought her too close to the shark's teeth. But this way…

"Sure, I'll help you," she said, pulling out a sheet of paper from the file drawer on her desk. "Let's start with the basics. Name, address, occupation."

He rattled off his address. "I believe you know the rest. Especially my name."

Her cheeks heated again when she thought of how she had whispered his first name back at the coffee shop, of the way that same syllable had echoed in her dreams, her thoughts. Oh, yeah, she knew his name. Too well. "Uh, date of birth?"

He gave her that, too, then grinned. "I'm a Taurus, or at least I think I am. And I like long walks on the beach and moonlit dances."

She snorted. "Whatever."

"Would you rather I said monster truck rallies and mud wrestling championships?"

She laughed. "Now *that* I would believe."

"Ah, then you don't know me very well." He leaned forward, propping his elbows on his knees. "I love the beach. I couldn't move away from the ocean if I tried. There's nothing like waking up on a warm Sunday morning, and having the ocean breeze coming in through your window."

"I like that, too," she said, then drew herself up. What was this, connect with Jack time? *Focus, Marnie, focus.* "Favorite music? Movies?"

"I like jazz. The kind of music that makes you think of smoky bars and good whiskey. Where you want to sit in a corner booth with a beautiful woman and listen to the band."

A beautiful woman like her? Marnie glanced down at the sheet, saw she had written the question, then scribbled it out. That made her twice as determined to get

Jack out of her life. Marnie Franklin didn't do scatter-brained or dreamy or infatuated. Damn. "Uh, movies?"

"I don't get to see many movies, and as much as I'd like to say something smart like *Requiem for a Dream*, I have to cave to a cliché. If you check my DVR, there's a lot of action movies on there." He shrugged. "What can I say? In a pinch, I opt for *The Terminator.*"

"I'll be baaack, huh?" she said, doing a pretty bad imitation of Arnold.

He chuckled. "Exactly. What about you? What's your favorite movie?"

"I cave to the cliché, too. Any kind of romantic comedy. Especially *You've Got Mail.*"

"Isn't that the one where the woman fell in love with her enemy?" Jack's blue eyes met hers, a tease winking in their ocean depths.

Did he know? Did he suspect her hidden agenda? Then he smiled and she relaxed. No. He didn't know who she really was or what she was planning for his "match." He'd been joking, not probing to see if this particular Romeo and Juliet had a shot.

She didn't care if they both liked the ocean, jazz music, and fun movies. If they'd both suffered a loss of a parent, and were still searching for something that would never be. He had ruined her life, her family. More than that, he was the kind of man who encouraged her to let loose, to become some giggly schoolgirl. She'd seen enough women make the mistake of leaping into a relationship without thinking, and refused to do the same. This wasn't a Nora Ephron movie—it was reality.

She glanced down at the paperwork. *Treat him like any other client,* she repeated. Again. "Uh, what about things to do? In your free time?"

"Running at the gym. Seeing outdoor concerts. Walking the streets of Boston."

She sighed, then put down the pen. "This isn't going to work if you keep flirting with me."

"I'm not flirting with you, Marnie. If I was flirting with you, you'd know it."

"That—" she waved a finger between them "—was definitely flirting."

"No. *This* is flirting." He got up again and approached her desk, then placed his hands on the oak surface and leaned over until their faces were inches apart. She caught the dark undertow of his cologne, the steady heat from his body. His blue eyes teemed with secrets. A lock of dark hair swooped across his brow. The crazy urge to brush it back rose in her chest.

"You are a beautiful, intoxicating, infuriating woman," he whispered, his voice a low, sensual growl, "and I can't stop thinking about you. And I love the way you look today. All…unfettered. Untamed."

Heat washed over her body, unfurled a deep, dark flame in her womb. She opened her mouth to speak, and for a moment, could only breathe and stare into those storm-tossed eyes of his. "Okay." Her words shook and she drew in a breath to steady herself. "Yes, that…that was flirting."

He smiled, held her gaze a moment longer, then retreated to the chair. "Glad we got that settled."

Settled? If anything, things between them had become more unsettled. A place Marnie never liked to be. Her concentration had flown south for the winter, and every thought in her head revolved around finding the nearest bedroom and taking her sweet time to "flirt" with Jack Knight.

Jack Knight. The enemy. In more ways than one.

She cleared her throat and retrieved her pen. In a normal client meeting, she'd let the questions flow in a natural rhythm. Her initial meetings were usually more like a chat with a new neighbor than a formal interview, but with Jack, she couldn't seem to form a coherent thought. "I, well, I think that's all I need for now. I'll be in touch in a couple days with some potential matches."

"That was easy. You sure you don't need anything else?"

You, a bedroom, more of those kisses. "Nope, I'm good," she said, too fast.

"Okay." He started to rise, and she put out a hand but didn't touch him.

She refused to let a silly thing like attraction get in the way of her goals. She needed information, and she needed Jack out of her life. Today. She could accomplish both right now.

Here was her opportunity to finally do what she'd been trying to do for weeks—find out about his business and how he operated. Maybe then she'd have the answers she needed, the ones that would close the hole in her heart and answer the what-ifs. She'd finally be able to accept the loss of her father, and move forward.

"Jack, wait a second. You know, lots of the women you'll be paired with work in complimentary fields. It might be good to get to know more about your job."

He sat back down. "Makes sense. I've told you a little about what I do. What else do you need to know?"

She had to word this carefully, or he'd realize she was looking for more than just matchmaking info. "Well, let's start with something general. Pretend we're chatting for the first time."

"Over coffee?" He grinned.

She hardened her features. The last thing she needed

to do was think about that walk to the coffee shop. Or the cookie crumb driven kiss. *Keep this professional.* "Or over a desk in an office."

He nodded agreement. "Okay, shoot."

"Tell me more about how you decide which companies to invest in and which ones you walk away from."

He cleared his throat and when he spoke again, the flirt had left his voice and he was all business. "A lot of that is a matter of numbers. I look at their market share, profit and loss, balance sheets, and weigh that against future potential and opportunities. If the dollars aren't there, it doesn't make financial sense for me to invest. But, sometimes I do anyway." He shrugged. "Because of the Caterpillar Factor."

"The Caterpillar Factor?" She stopped writing. "I've never heard of that before."

"It's something I made up. When you buy a business, there's a lot of data to wade through. But in the end, I let my instincts make the final decision. That's the Caterpillar Factor." He leaned forward in the chair, his eyes bright with enthusiasm. "You know how you can look at a caterpillar and get grossed out by it? I mean, most of them are fat and have a bunch of legs, and aren't exactly something you want crawling on you."

"That's true." She gave an involuntary shudder.

"But those same caterpillars have the *potential* to be something really incredible. When you look at them, you don't know what it will be—you're judging it entirely on its current form. But underneath, buried deep inside that caterpillar, is something that, given enough time and nurturing, will be amazing and beautiful."

"A butterfly," she said, her voice quiet.

"Exactly." He grinned. "Not every business is a butterfly waiting to be unveiled, but some are. And I know that by investing in and coaching them, I can help them become something amazing." He gave a little nod, and a flush crept into his cheeks. "I know, it sounds kind of corny."

She never would have thought she'd see Jack Knight embarrassed or shy or vulnerable. But here he was, admitting that he believed in potential, that he sometimes went with his gut, even against conventional wisdom. Wasn't that how she approached her matchmaking? No computer algorithms, no formulas, just instinct?

Why did this one man—the wrong man—discombobulate her so? She'd never met anyone who could do that with nothing more than a smile, a whisper of her name.

Damn it all. She related to him, understood him, and that added another complicated layer to what she'd thought would be a simple matter of revenge. The closer they got to each other, the more she allowed him to burrow his way into her heart, the harder it became to implement her plan.

She glanced down at the paper before her. The words swam in her vision. Why hadn't Jack seen a butterfly in Top Notch Printing, her father's business? Why hadn't he helped her father more? Wasn't Tom Franklin's life and livelihood worth some time and nurturing, too?

"And what about the ones that won't be butterflies? What do you do with those businesses?"

He sighed. "Sometimes, the business is too far gone, or the owner just isn't equipped with the right skill set to help it reach the next level. We could throw millions at the company and it wouldn't be enough. In those cases, we sell off the parts, recoup our investment, and hopefully send the owner off with cash in his pocket."

"Hopefully?" The word squeaked past the tension in her jaw.

"You're a businesswoman, Marnie. I'm sure you understand that there are a million factors that can affect the decision to keep or sell a company. Some owners are great at running a business, some…aren't."

She thought of her affable, fun-loving father. He'd never been much for keeping track of paperwork or receipts. Never one to demand a late payment or argue with a customer. But that meant Tom had needed more help, not less. Why hadn't Jack seen that?

"Sometimes, despite all the due diligence in the world," Jack said, "we make mistakes, and sometimes life throws us a curveball that we didn't expect. A supplier goes under or a major customer takes their sales elsewhere. Sometimes, the companies recoup, sometimes…"

"They die," she finished. She had to swallow hard and remind herself to keep breathing.

He nodded. "Yeah, they do."

"You seem awful cavalier about this." As if there weren't people hurt in the process. As if the only thing that died was a bottom line. She clenched her hands together under her desk, feigning a calm she didn't feel.

"It's a reality. Fifty percent of businesses fail, for a million reasons. You can pump all the cash you want into them, and some just aren't destined to survive. If I got emotional about each one, I'd get distracted and lose sight of the big picture. So I don't make my decisions based on emotion. I think it helps that I don't exactly love my job, but I…respect it. Maybe someday down the road, I'll get a chance to do something else."

"And what is the big picture? Profits?"

"Well, everyone likes to make money. But for me,

it's the businesses I see succeed. Like Dot's coffee shop or my friend Toby's gym. I see the placed filled with happy customers, and that tells me I did the right thing. It's not about profits, it's about quality of life. For the owners, and their clients."

"And the businesses that don't make it?" she said. "What are they to you?"

"The cost of doing business. It sounds harsh, but in the end, when there's nothing more that can be done, a failure is reduced to dollars and cents."

Under the desk, her hands curled into fists. She worked a smile to her face, even though it hurt. The smile, and the truth. "Well, I guess that's all I need."

Please leave, please get out of here before my heart breaks right in front of you.

The chips from earlier churned in her gut. She wished her day was over, because right now, all she wanted to do was go home, draw the shades, and stay in bed.

Not only had Jack just confirmed that her father's business had been a negative number in the general ledger, but his asking her to find him a match confirmed she was a negative in his personal ledger, too. This was what she'd wanted—the truth and to be rid of Jack. But still, the success had a bitter taste.

"Thanks again for taking the time to see me today, Marnie." Jack got to his feet. "I look forward to hearing from you, and seeing who you match me up with." He looked like he wanted to say something more, but all he said was goodbye before heading for the door. One hand on the knob, he turned back. "You know, you should let your hair down more often. And I mean that, literally and figuratively. It suits you. Very nicely."

The door shut behind him with a soft click. Marnie

sat in her chair, watching the space for a long time. She shook off the maudlin thoughts and turned to her contacts database. Jack Knight had asked her for a match, and she intended to give him one—

A match that would challenge him and keep him far from Marnie.

Then maybe he'd stop flirting with her, and tipping her carefully constructed life upside-down. Because there was one thing she knew for sure. Jack Knight was bad for business—the business of Marnie's heart.

CHAPTER SIX

JACK KNIGHT WAS rarely wrong. He had learned over the years to read people's body language, the subtle clues they sent out that created a roadmap to their thoughts and actions. He'd used that skill a thousand times in negotiations, and in strategic meetings. But when it came to Marnie Franklin, his instincts had failed him, big time. He'd completely underestimated how angry she was—

And how far he was from proving himself as a different man than his father.

He strode into her office a week after their last meeting, waving off the assistant's offer to help him, heading straight for Marnie's desk. "What kind of match was that?"

"What are you talking about?"

"That date you set me up on. What were you thinking?"

She leaned an elbow on her chair, relaxed, unconcerned. Her eyes widened as he approached, then a flicker of a smile appeared on her face and disappeared just as fast. A smile like she knew what she had done. "I'm sorry you're unhappy with the Matchmaking by Marnie match, but we truly thought—"

"*Unhappy?* I wouldn't say that. The woman was nice

and very energetic, but not my type, at all." His gaze narrowed. "Did you do that on purpose?"

"I have no idea what you're talking about," Marnie said. With a straight face.

"Marnie, I have to go to that meeting with the caterer," her assistant said. "But if you want, I'll stay awhile longer."

"I'll be fine. Go ahead to the appointment, Erica." Marnie waved her off.

Erica, Marnie's sister. His gaze skipped to her, and he saw the same leery look in her eyes as in Marnie's. Oh, yeah, they knew who he was here—or who they thought he was. Damn. How was he going to prove the opposite?

Once the door shut behind Erica, Jack winnowed the space between himself and Marnie's desk. She looked beautiful today, her hair up in its perpetual clip, her button down white shirt pressed and neat, accented by a simple gold chain and form fitting black skirt.

"I'm sure Miss Stewart will be a great match for someone, but that someone isn't me."

"You just have to give her a chance," Marnie said. "Roberta…takes some time to get to know."

"Oh, I think she's a great person. We went out dancing, and even though I run four days a week, she outdanced me ten to one. And she's funny and enthusiastic, but not my type. What did you think we'd have in common?"

Marnie shrugged. Played innocent. "Sometimes opposites attract."

"And sometimes matchmakers don't play fair. I came to you as a legitimate client—"

"No, you didn't." She got to her feet, and her features shifted from detachment to fire. He could see it in the way her eyes flashed, her lips narrowed. "You might have said you wanted a match, but it didn't take a rocket scientist to figure out your true motive. You came here, hoping I'd think you were my perfect match."

"You have made it abundantly clear that you are not interested in me. That's why I think you should put your money where your mouth is."

"What is that supposed to mean?"

"You go out with me on a real date."

"Why would I do that?"

"Because despite your strong efforts in the opposite direction—" and thinking of the mismatch she'd sent him, he wondered if it wasn't just revenge but that deep down inside, Marnie didn't want to see him connect with another woman "—I think we'd be a great match."

She scoffed. "That's my job, not yours."

"And yet you have not found the perfect man for you." He leaned on her desk and met her green eyes. "Why is that?"

"I...I work a lot. I haven't had time to date."

"Is that all? Time? Because it's the end of the day. We could make time right now."

"Go out with you? Now?"

He grinned. "Why wait?"

"I am not interested in dating you. Ever."

"What was that walk to coffee? To me, it was a trial date."

She snorted. "There's no such thing."

He leaned in closer, until her eyes widened and that intoxicating perfume she wore teased at his senses. "We don't have to follow the rules, Marnie. We can make them up as we go along."

Her mouth opened, closed. She inhaled, and for a second, he thought she'd agree. A smile started to curve up his face, when he noticed the fire return to her green eyes. "I only have one rule. To stay far away from you." She got out of her seat, standing tall in her heels and matching him in height. "Don't think another Franklin will fall for your line of bull again, Jack. You don't get to ruin any more lives in this family. We're done believing in your lies and your charming little pep talks. So stay far away from this family."

And there it was. The past he couldn't run from, sweep under a rug, or ignore. Guilt rocketed through him. If Marnie knew how much of a hand Jack had had in her father's business closing, she'd never forgive him. He wanted her to see him as the man he was today, not the man he used to be, but getting from A to B meant confronting A and dealing with it, once and for all. "Yes, we did work with your father and his shop. And I swear, I had no idea you were his daughter until you told me your nickname. He always called you Daisy when he talked about you."

Hurt flickered in her eyes. "That business would still be operating today under Tom Franklin," Marnie said, the words biting, cold. "If someone didn't destroy it."

"Marnie, there's more to it than that. I—"

"I have no interest in anything you have to say to me, or any claims you intend to make about your 'business practices,'" Marnie said. "My sisters and I watched our father fall apart after you stepped in and 'helped' him. You. Ruined. Him. And helped him…" she bit her lip, and tears welled in her eyes "…die too soon."

"Marnie, I didn't do that." But he had, hadn't he? He'd talked Tom into signing on the dotted line, knowing full well what the true intent of Knight would be. And when Tom needed a friend, Jack was gone. *You're a cold, uninvolved man, Jack.* "I mean, yes, I did invest in your father's business, and yes, I did counsel him, but—"

"Get out of my office," Marnie said, waving toward the door, her face tight with rage. "And don't ever come back. I don't want to hear any more of your lies and I sure as hell don't want to date you."

He opened his mouth, but she pointed at the door again. "For someone who's perfected the art of matching people, you of all people should understand that some matches go well and some don't. It takes two to make it work. And sometimes only one to destroy it."

"Yeah, you."

He took her anger, and let it wash over him. He understood now why she had bristled every time he talked about his job. Why she had been so warm at first, then so cold. And why she had set him up on a date that was bound not to work out. "Sometimes," he said quietly, "our best intentions can go down paths we never saw. I'm sorry, Marnie, about your father and his business. If I could change any of it, I would."

Then he left, and for the first time since he'd taken over Knight Enterprises, he wished for a do-over. Another chance to go back and do a better job.

Her mother had canceled Tuesday night dinner at her house, Thursday night's card game, and Saturday's brunch. And now, the morning after the confrontation with Jack in Marnie's office, Helen was trying to get out of her regular Wednesday lunch with Marnie. "Ma, I haven't seen you in two weeks," Marnie said.

"I'm sorry, honey. We've just been so busy, going to the ball games and Bingo and…"

While her mother talked, Marnie debated the best way to tell her mother the truth. She'd spent a sleepless night debating the pros and cons of telling Helen the truth about Jack, but in the end, there was only one option.

Put it out there, and let the consequences fall as they may.

Her family had never been one to tackle the hard topics. They'd put a sunny face on everything, and done a good job avoiding. This, though, they couldn't avoid any longer—because Helen was falling hard for Dan.

Marnie hated being in this position. Standing in the middle of two evils, both of which would hurt the ones she loved. She'd thought that standing up to Jack and telling him how she felt would make her feel better. But instead of relieving the anger and betrayal in her gut, the confrontation had left her restless, replaying every word a hundred times in her head.

No. She'd done the right thing. Now she needed to do the right thing again—

And break her mother's heart.

"Dan and I have just been having so much fun," Helen said. "Oh, did I tell you, he's taking me to Maine for the weekend on Friday? He found this lovely little cottage in Kennebunkport. If we get lucky, maybe we'll even see the former president on the beach."

That meant they were getting serious. Damn. Marnie had hoped the relationship between Dan and her mother would fizzle, saving Marnie from having to tell her mother the truth about who Dan was.

She'd avoided the truth forever, but where had that gotten her? Nowhere good. And it had given her mother and Dan time to get closer, which only added more complications. Marnie took a deep breath. "Are you free for lunch today, Ma? I'll stop on the way to get us some Thai food, if you want."

"That sounds wonderful."

Marnie said goodbye, then powered through the rest of her morning appointments, keeping her head on her job instead of what was to come. Lord, how she dreaded this. Her mother had sounded so happy, with that little laugh in her voice that they had all missed over the last few years. And now Marnie was about to erase it all.

But as she got closer to Ma's house, and the scent of the Thai food overpowered the interior of the car, Marnie wanted to turn around. To delay again. It wasn't just about breaking her mother's heart anymore, but about facing the truth herself. All along, she kept hoping to be wrong about Jack. To find out that the guy with the amazing smile and earth-shattering kisses wasn't the evil vulture she'd painted him to be.

But he was, and the sooner she got that cemented in her mind, the better.

Even if the man had asked her out. Why would he do that? Was he truly interested? Or was she just another conquest?

Helen greeted her daughter with a big hug, and a thousand-miles-an-hour of chatter about Dan. "He's just the sweetest guy, Marnie. I can't believe no one has scooped him up. He holds the door for me, brings me flowers, even sings to me." She smiled, one of those soft, quiet smiles. "I really like him."

Guilt washed over Marnie. "Ma, we need to talk. Come on, let's go in the kitchen."

A few minutes later, both women had steaming plates of pad thai in front of them, but no one was eating. "Okay, shoot. What did you want to tell me?" Helen asked.

"Dan isn't...who you think he is," Marnie said, the words hurting her throat. "I should have caught this when I interviewed him, but to be honest, I never ask about kids or stepkids and—"

"What do you mean? I've met Dan's stepson. Remember? After the mixer. He seemed very nice—"

"He's Jack Knight."

Helen froze. "Jack Knight? That's impossible. Dan's last name is Simpson."

"He's his stepfather. Jack is the owner of Knight Enterprises. The same Knight Enterprises that destroyed Dad's business. If you keep dating Dan, you'll be seeing Jack, and the reminder of everything that happened to Dad. I'm so sorry to have to tell you this."

Silence filled the kitchen, and the food grew cold on their plates. Helen got to her feet, waving off her daughter. Ma crossed to the sink, placed her hands on either side of the porcelain basin and stood there a long time, her gaze going to the garden outside the window. The rain pelted soft knocks on the glass, then slid down in little shimmering rivers.

"Ma?" Marnie said. She walked over to her mother, and placed a hand on Helen's shoulder. "Ma, I'm so sorry. If I had known, I never would have fixed him up with you."

"Dan is the best thing to come along in my life in a really long time," Helen said, her voice thick with emotion that made Marnie's guilt factor rocket upward. "Besides you girls, of course." She closed her hand around Marnie's, and gave her daughter a smile. "I'm glad I met him."

"He is a great guy, I agree, and if he wasn't related to Jack—"

"It doesn't matter. Dan and I are happy. I don't care who his stepson is." Helen turned around and placed her back against the sink. Her features had shifted from heartbreak to determination. "We might work out, we might not, but we're going to give it a shot. Life's too short, honey, and I don't want to spend any more of my time alone."

This was a new Helen, Marnie realized. A woman who hadn't been defeated by the loss of her husband, and the prospect of starting her life over again, but rather energized by it. She also showed an amazing strength that had probably always been there, waiting for the right moment to appear. Dating Dan had only emphasized those qualities, not detracted.

Her mother was happy. Taking chances. Making changes. Jumping into the unknown. All things that Marnie had held back from doing, sticking to her organized planner and her rigid schedule.

Still, the urge to protect her mother, to head off any further hurt, rose in Marnie. If Dan and Helen stayed together, it would be nothing but a constant reminder, a cut against an old scab, again and again.

"I just don't want you to be hurt again," Marnie said.

"If there's one thing I've finally learned and accepted, it's that life comes with hurt. But if you're willing to risk that, you can find such amazing happiness, too."

On the wall, one of those kitschy cat shaped wall clocks clicked its tail back and forth with the passing seconds. Helen gestured toward the black plastic body, a stark contrast to the pin-neat, granite and white kitchen. "Do you remember when your father got me that?"

Marnie smiled. "It was a joke Christmas gift. We never thought you'd hang it up."

"It made me laugh. It makes me laugh every time I see it on the wall. That's why I hung it up, and why I kept it there, to remember to have fun sometimes."

"But isn't that the problem?" Marnie said, the words tumbling out of her mouth before she could stop them. "We're always having fun, never talking about the hard stuff. You can't just keep ignoring the facts, Ma."

Helen's soft hands cupped her daughter's face. "Oh, Marnie, Marnie. My serious one. Always trying so hard to keep the rest of us in line."

"I just like things to…stay ordered."

"And our lives when you were younger were far from ordered, weren't they? But we had fun, oh, how we had fun. Your father never had a serious day in his life, bless his heart." Helen released Marnie and the two women retook their seats at the table. "Let's talk about Knight and your father. And what really happened."

All these years, they'd avoided the subject. Whenever it came up, her mother would say she couldn't bear to hear it, and they'd switch to something inane or trivial. But this new Helen, the one who had been tempered by life on her own, had a determination in her eyes and voice that surprised Marnie.

"What do you know about what happened to Dad's company?" Ma said.

"Knight Enterprises invested in the company at first, made big promises about helping him get it profitable again, then deserted him and let him fail. When the business went south, Dad sold the rest of it to them for a fraction of what it was worth." Marnie bit back a curse. "And after that, Dad just…gave up."

"Part of that's true." Helen laid her hands on top of each other on the table. She smiled. "You and I are so much alike, Marnie. We both try to keep the peace, keep everyone happy. Sometimes, you need to rock the boat and tell the truth."

Marnie knew what was coming before her mother

spoke. She'd probably always known, but like her mother, found it easier to pin her anger on Jack, rather than accept the facts.

"That business was on its last legs before your father went to Knight for help. Tom had lost his passion for it years earlier, and in the last couple of years before he sold, he'd spent too many days going fishing on the boat instead of working. A business is like a garden. You have to keep tending it, or it'll die on the vine. And your father stopped tending it." She shrugged. "I knew, but I figured we were okay. And I couldn't blame him. He'd worked so many hours when he first started out and he hated being the boss. The one to hire, fire, and demand. Plus, he missed you girls' soccer games and softball matches, and weekend family trips. I think he just wanted a break, to live his life before he got too old to do so and..."

Her voice trailed off and she bit her lip. "He just wanted time. With his family. With the people most important to him. There was a lot involved in that decision, Marnie. A lot you didn't know. Your father kept things to himself, hated to worry us. All he kept saying was that we'd be fine."

"Keeping the sunshine on his face," Marnie said, repeating her father's oft-used phrase.

"That was his philosophy, right or wrong. And so I couldn't blame him for wanting time to enjoy his days. He said he had put money aside for retirement, and that we would be all right once he got some investors on board. The company would turn around, freeing him up. We'd have time together, we'd travel, we'd treat you girls to all those extras we hadn't been able to afford before. I trusted him. I'd been married to the man nearly all my life, why wouldn't I?"

Marnie's jaw dropped as she put the pieces together. The financial struggle her mother had had over the last few years, her decision to go back to work. "There was no retirement?"

Helen shook her head, sad and slow. "Your father had spent it all, investing it in some fishing charter thing his cousin Rick talked him into, and kept telling him it would pay off. Just be patient, wait, and your dad did. Too long."

Her father, a trusting, optimistic man, who had trusted a family member when he should have had his guard up. In the end, it didn't surprise Marnie as much as reveal a different side of her father.

"Rick's business went belly up before it started, and the money was gone," Ma said. "Our entire future, gone in an instant. All our equity. All we had left was the house and the company, which by then wasn't worth much at all."

"So he sold a majority interest in the business to get the money back," Marnie finished.

Helen nodded. "Your father partnered with Knight on the agreement that they would be there to provide counsel to help him get the printing company back on track. They talked about bringing in an expert to help the operation get leaner, more efficient, hire some sales people to generate more income. Tom thought maybe he could bring about a financial miracle before I realized what happened to the retirement money. But then Knight didn't help. As soon as the paperwork was signed, the help and advice stopped. And the company, like you said, faltered. When Knight came back and offered to buy the remaining assets, your father jumped at the offer, even though it meant taking a loss. By then, he knew there was no way to rebound, and I don't think he had the heart or desire to put in the hours that might take. He wanted to be here, not behind that desk. Still, your father felt so guilty, and I think that's what broke his heart in the end. I had no idea. If I had…" She shook her head, regrets clouding her eyes. "He didn't tell me any of this until shortly before he died. I wish he'd told me sooner. Oh, how I wish he had. Communication was never the strong suit in this family, and we had…so many other worries at the time. If he'd said something—"

"We would have stepped in and helped," Marnie said. "I would have gone to work for him or loaned him some money or…" She paused as the realization dawned in her mind. Her father, sacrificing for his family right to the end. "That's why he didn't tell us. He didn't want us to do any of that."

Helen's soft palm cupped her daughter's cheek. "He was so proud of you. You and your sisters. You found jobs that you love, that speak to your heart, and he would never have asked you to give that up."

"But, Ma, we could have helped him. Done something."

"And it would have made him miserable. He wanted you girls to be happy in your own lives, not make up for his mistakes. Not to worry about him all the time."

"He wasn't perfect," Marnie said, "but he sure was a great dad."

"Before he died, he made me promise not to let hurt or anger fill my heart. That's why he got me that clock the last Christmas before he died. So I'd remember to be happy, to tick along. To not let what happened ruin our future." Her mother got to her feet, took the clock off the wall and pressed it into Marnie's hands. "Take this, hang it on your wall, and remember to be happy, Marnie. To be silly. And most of all, to forgive."

The two of them hugged, two women who had lost a man they loved, and who shared common regrets. Outside, the rain washed over the house, washed it clean, and inside the kitchen, the first steps of healing truly began.

CHAPTER SEVEN

"TELL ME AGAIN why I'm here, besides serving as a fifth wheel," Jack said. They were standing in the lobby of a seafood restaurant located on the wharf. In the distance, he could hear the clanging of the buoys. The scent of the ocean, salty, tangy, carried on the air, a perfect complement to the restaurant's menu.

Dan chuckled. "I thought it'd be nice for you to get to know Helen a little better. And it'll do you good to eat a meal that doesn't come out of a takeout box."

Jack grinned. "You have a point there."

"Parents are always right. Just remember that." Dan arched a brow, a smirk on his face. The door to the restaurant opened, and Helen strode in, shaking off the rain on her coat and her umbrella. Her gaze met Dan's and a smile sparked on her face.

A wave of jealousy washed over Jack. Not that he begrudged Dan a moment of happiness, but seeing Helen's happiness, and the echoing emotion in his stepfather, was a stark reminder to Jack of his solitary life.

"Did you tell him?" Helen asked.

"Nope." Dan grinned again.

That didn't sound good. Jack sent Dan an inquisitive look. "Tell me what?"

Then the door to the restaurant opened again and

Marnie walked in. At first, she was too busy brushing off the rain to notice Jack. She shrugged out of her raincoat, handing it the coat check. Then she turned, and his groin tightened, his pulse skipped a beat and everything within him sprang to attention. Wow.

Marnie had on a clingy dark green dress that accented the blond in her hair, made her eyes seem bigger, more luminous. The dress skimmed her body, showed off her arms, her incredible legs, and dropped in an enticing V in the front.

She smiled when she saw Dan and her mother. Then her gaze swiveled to Jack and the smile disappeared. "Why are you here?"

"I was invited," he said.

"So was I." She tipped her head toward her mother. "Ma?"

Helen took Dan's arm and beamed at both Jack and Marnie. "Our table's ready. Let's go have dinner."

"Ma—"

"Come on, Marnie, Jack." Then Helen turned on her heel and headed into the dining room with Dan, leaving Jack and Marnie two choices—follow or walk out the door. Marnie looked ready to do the latter.

Jack tossed Marnie a grin. "It is their treat, and we do need to eat. Should we call a truce, for the sake of our parents?"

She hesitated, biting her lower lip, then nodded. "If they stay together we'll inevitably see each other once in a while. So we should at least get along tonight. For their sake."

"*If* they stay together? I thought you were the best matchmaker around," he teased. "Hmmm…maybe you were wrong about who you matched me with, too."

"You were a special case."

He laughed. "Now that I agree with."

She rolled her eyes, but a slight smile played on her lips. It was enough. It gave Jack hope that maybe, just maybe, all was not lost between them. She strode into the dining room, with him bringing up the rear.

They sat across from Dan and Helen, who had taken seats together on one side of the table. Another element of Dan and Helen's strategic plan, one Jack had to admit he admired. The waiter took their drink orders, left them with menus, then headed off to the bar.

"I'm glad you both decided to join us for dinner," Helen said.

Dan draped an arm over the back of Helen's chair and she shifted a bit closer to him. "We figured it would take a miracle for you two to see you're as matched as two peas in a pod—"

"Dad—"

Dan put up a hand. "Hear me out, Jack. Marnie's mother and I are pretty damned happy. And we want to see both of you just as happy as we are. Now, maybe you two won't work out. But you'll never know unless you give it a chance."

"You had to get your matchmaking abilities somewhere," Helen said to Marnie. "Dare I suggest your mother's side of the family?"

"They're pretty obvious," Marnie said to Jack.

He nodded, a smirk on his face. "Maybe they've got something here."

Dan and Helen watched the exchange with amusement. "Like I said, you should always listen to your parents," Dan said. "We've got age and experience on our side."

"Definitely the latter," Helen said with a flirtatious tone in her voice. She flushed, then laughed, and gave

Dan a quick kiss on his cheek. He cupped her face, and kissed her again.

A craving for that—that happiness, that ease with another person, that loving attention—rose in Marnie fast and fierce. Her mother had taken this leap, taken the biggest risk of all and fallen for someone else. Could Marnie do the same?

If she didn't, she knew she'd never have what her mother had right now. And oh, how Marnie wanted it. More than she ever had before.

She slid a glance in Jack's direction. Every woman with a pulse had noticed him tonight. He had on a dark blue pinstripe suit, a pale blue shirt the color of the sky on a cold morning, and a green and silver striped tie that coordinated with her dress, as if they'd planned it that way. His dark hair seemed to beg for her to run her fingers through it, while the sharp lines of his jaw urged her to kiss him.

If he was any other man, and she was any other woman, she would want him. She would probably date him. Fall for him. But even the thought of that caused the familiar panic to rise inside her chest.

Falling for Jack would be like jumping off a cliff. It was the kind of heady rush that Marnie avoided at all costs. Not to mention, his mere presence was a constant reminder of what had happened to her father's business. She couldn't do that to herself, but most especially, to her mother or sisters.

"It's very sweet of you both to think we should date," Marnie said, "but this matchmaker doesn't see the logic in that. Jack and I are too…different."

Helen propped her chin on her hands. "Really? Different? How?"

Marnie shifted in her seat. "He's a businessman—"

"As are you."

"Well, I'm in a creative industry. He's...corporate."

"That just means you'll compliment each other's skills," Helen said.

Dan nodded. "Yup. Like ranch dressing and celery sticks."

Jack turned in his chair and put one arm on the back. "There are the things we have in common, too. Like music. Hobbies."

"Not movies," she pointed out, then felt silly for even mentioning it. Really? Her strongest argument was that Jack liked *The Terminator* and she liked tissue-ready chick flicks?

Jack nodded and feigned deep thought. "There is that. Well, that settles it, then."

She breathed a sigh of relief. Good. He wasn't going along with this charade any more than she was. "Great."

"We just won't watch movies," he said, then leaned toward her. His dark, woodsy cologne teased at her senses, urged her to come closer, to nuzzle his neck, taste his lips. "We'll find other ways to entertain ourselves."

Desire roared through Marnie's veins, an instant, insane tsunami of want, as if Jack had reached over, and flicked a switch to On. Across from them, Dan laughed, and Helen gave them a knowing smile.

"I, uh, forgot. I have a meeting with a client." Marnie grabbed her purse and jerked to her feet. The only thing she could do to avoid this disaster was to leave. "I'm so sorry. Maybe we could do this another time."

Helen apologized to the men, then headed out after her daughter.

After the women had left, Dan turned to his stepson

and sighed. "Sorry, son. We thought that would work out better than it did."

"It's okay. She can't forgive me for what Knight did to her father's company. I understand that." Heck, he heard it every day, as he worked to make amends, to try to undo the damage that had been done both by his father and himself.

But there were days when the task felt like pushing back a wall of water. He'd think he was making progress, then unearth another stack of files or get another phone call from a lawyer and realize how far he had yet to go. In between, he was still running Knight Enterprises, and still working on investment deals and helping the businesses he funded. A Herculean task, even with a staff working along with him.

"She'll come around," Dan said. "Look at the people you have helped. You've gotten, what, twenty companies back up and running? Invested in another dozen business owners whose companies had been dissolved? You've got a gift there, son, and you're using it to do good. I'm proud of you."

The tender words warmed Jack. For so long, he had wanted to hear them from his biological father, but never had, even when he'd modeled Jack, Senior's ruthless behavior. Now, in doing the opposite of his biological dad, he had earned respect and pride from the man who had truly been his father, with or without a DNA connection. And that, in the end, meant far more to Jack. His biological father might never have appreciated or understood or supported him, but this man did all three, and that was the mark of a true parent. "Thanks, Dad. That means a lot."

Jack's gaze went to the restaurant exit. A part of him

hoped like hell that Marnie had changed her mind, but no, Helen was making her way back to the table. Alone.

"And don't you worry about Marnie," Dan said as if he'd read his stepson's mind. "You'll figure out the best way to win her heart because that's your specialty. Solving the big problems and creating a happy ending for everyone."

Jack thought of the piles of folders on his credenza. The companies he had yet to find a way to restore or repair. He had a way to go, a hell of a long way to go, in creating those happy endings. And judging by the way Marnie had looked at him tonight, he had a way to go in the romantic happy ending department, too. It was time to admit defeat and quit chasing something that didn't want to be caught.

"If there's one thing I've learned in business, it's when to walk away from the deal," Jack said, getting to his feet, and nodding a goodbye to his stepfather and Helen. "And when it's time to move on to another candidate."

Every time Marnie managed to put him from her mind, Jack Knight popped back into her world, a few days after the dinner with her mother and Dan. Marnie had just locked the door on the office and turned toward home, exhausted and beyond ready for a vacation, or at the very least a weekend away from the calls and emails and meetings, when a familiar silver car pulled into the lot and Jack hopped out of the driver's seat. The trunk had been restored to new condition, all evidence of the wreck erased by some talented body shop.

As for Jack, despite everything, a little thrill ran through her at the sight of him, tall and lean, in a pair of well-worn jeans, a cotton button-down and a dark brown sports jacket. He looked…comfortable. Sexy. Like a man she could lean into and the world would drop away.

"Leaving so soon?" Jack asked.

"It's nearly noon," she said. "On a Sunday. Most people left the office two days ago."

"Just us workaholics still in the city, huh?" He reached into his jacket and withdrew a bright pink flyer. "And people planning on going to the Esplanade this afternoon to soak up some sun and hear the MAJE Jazz Showcase."

"What's that?"

"Top scoring high school bands from around the area get to perform at the Hatch Shell every year. And this year, my cousin is playing in one of the bands that won gold at the state competition, which automatically puts the band into the showcase." He took a couple steps closer to her. "How about it? Would you like to go and support the local arts?"

"Me? Why?"

"Because I think you would enjoy it. We both like jazz, and it's a gorgeous day, one we should take advantage of and spend a few hours enjoying. And—" he took a couple steps closer to her "—because I am officially asking you on a real date."

"Jack—"

"You know, after that dinner at the restaurant, I told myself to walk away. To quit pursuing someone who didn't want to be pursued. And I did. But you know what the problem with my theory is?"

She shook her head.

"I couldn't get you out of my mind. Maybe this is crazy. Maybe this is a really bad idea." He took another step closer, and his cologne teased her nostrils, and her pulse began to race. "But I want to see you again, Marnie."

That sent a zing through her heart, and a smile to her lips. "You are a stubborn man, Jack Knight." No one had ever pursued her this hard before, and if she was honest with herself, it was nice. Very nice.

A part of her wanted to run, to retreat to her familiar comfort of organization and schedules. But the other part of her, the part that had seen hundreds of happy couples walk down the aisle, wanted to take a chance. To trust in the very process she had built her business upon.

Still, she hesitated. This was Jack Knight, she reminded herself. Going out with him would only complicate an already complicated situation. Could hurt those she loved. "I should get home. It's my only day off—"

"And yet you were working."

"Well, my only *half* day off. I have laundry and other things to do."

"Wouldn't you rather grab a picnic lunch, spread a blanket on the grass at the Esplanade, and listen to some really amazing jazz?" he said, his voice like a siren calling to the part of her that craved a break, and the need for more in her life than her work. "Enjoy the beautiful spring day, maybe have a glass of wine, and just...be?"

God, yes, she wanted that. She relaxed far too little, worked far too much. Work kept her from thinking, though, and also prevented her from dwelling on her regrets. Oh, how tempting—and wrong—Jack's offer sounded.

Yet at the same time, he was a man who personified the very thing she avoided—taking risks. Trusting in others. Letting down your guard.

"That walk we took the other day did me some good,

too, and I'm not just talking about in a cardiovascular way," he said. "Sometimes, I need to be forced out the door or I work too many hours. This weekend, the geeks are doing some maintenance on the server. That means I can't work, not while the computers are down. And my cousin is really counting on me to be there. I couldn't bear to let him down." Jack grinned.

Why did he have to keep being so nice? So…normal?

She kept waiting to see the side of him that had swooped down and shredded her father's company, and she hadn't. Now here he was, admitting he was a workaholic like her, striking yet another sympathetic chord in her heart. One who, like her, also spent far too little time in the sun and with close family. She liked him, damn it, and really didn't want to.

She shook her head even as her resistance eroded a little more. "You don't need my company to do that."

"Ah, but a day like today is so much better when it's enjoyed with someone else, don't you agree?" He reached back and opened the rear passenger door of his car. "I already have a picnic and a blanket ready to go."

"So sure I was going to say yes?"

"Quite the opposite. I wanted to sweeten the pot because I knew you'd say no."

He could have read her mind. Five minutes ago, she'd written "take some time off" on a Post-It note and tacked it onto her desk, a reminder to stop working seven days, to have some time to regroup, recharge. Except for her thrice-weekly runs at the gym, there'd been far too much work and far too little relaxation in her days. In her business, a tired matchmaker wasn't as inspired when it came to putting matches together, hence the reminder for time off.

But a picnic with Jack? How could that be a good

choice? He was the kind of man who tempted her to take the very risks she'd avoided all her life. The kind of man who came with heartbreak written all over his face.

The kind of man she tried so very hard to resist. And failed.

She peered past him, and into the car. A bright green reusable shopping bag sat on top of a folded red plaid blanket. The shopping bag bulged, and the amber neck of a bottle of white wine stuck out of the top, alongside a spray of daisies.

Daisies.

Not roses. Not carnations. Not orchids. Daisies, their bright white faces so friendly and inviting.

Jack caught where her gaze had gone, and he reached inside, tugged out the flowers, and presented them to her. "I thought an unconventional woman deserved an unconventional flower."

She took them, and despite everything, her defensive walls against Jack melted a little more. "Did my mother tell you these were my favorites?"

"Nope. You did. When you told me about your nickname."

He'd remembered that tidbit. It touched her more than she wanted to admit. She fingered one of the blooms, and a smile curved across her face. "Every time I see daisies, they bring back great memories."

"Tell me," Jack said, his voice quiet and soft.

She inhaled the light scent of the delicate flowers. "When I was a little girl, there was a field near my house where daisies grew wild. Every spring, I couldn't wait for them to bloom. Once they did, I'd go and gather as many as I could carry and bring them to my mother. She'd arrange them in this big green vase of my grandmother's, set it in the center of the dining room table, and every night over dinner, we'd give one of the daisies a name. She said they have so much personality, they deserve to have their own names."

Jack leaned forward, and ran a finger along the delicate petals of one of the flowers. "And what's this one's name?"

She shook her head. "Jack, I'm too old for that."

"We both are. But it's fun to be young once in a while, don't you think? Believe me, I wish I'd taken more time to be a kid when I had the chance."

She heard something in his voice, something sad, regretful. She wondered again about the Jack Knight she thought she knew—who had ruined her father's company—and the Jack Knight she had met—a man with a definite soft spot. Which was the real Jack? Curiosity nudged her closer to him. "Why didn't you have more kid time?"

"Long, involved, unhappy story. I'll tell it to you if I'm ever on Oprah." He shook off the moment of somberness, then plucked one of the daisies from their paper wrapper. "I'm calling this one Fred."

She shook her head, stepping away. "Jack—"

He plucked a second flower from the arrangement and held it out to her. "Let go of all those rules and regulations you live by, Marnie."

"How do you know I do that?"

"Because we're two peas in a pod, as my stepfather would say. I have kept such a tight leash on everything in my life, trying to make up for the past, trying not to be the man my father was. And where has it gotten me? Working too many hours, eating most of my meals on the run, and living the same lonely work-centered life he lived."

"I'm not..." She shook her head, unable to complete the sentence.

Jack touched her cheek, his blue eyes soft, understanding. "I see a woman who works too much and plays too little. As if she's afraid to go after the very thing she helps her clients find."

It was as if he'd pulled open a curtain in Marnie's brain. How many times had she thought the same thing? Heard those same words from her sisters, her mom? She glanced at the daisies and saw her younger self in those happy white circles. When had she gotten away from that carefree person? When had she become this woman too scared to take a chance on love?

She reached out and took the flower, caught in the game, in Jack's infectious smile, in the echoing need to forget her adult problems for just a little while. "That makes this one Ethel."

"Sounds perfect, Marnie." He closed his hand over hers, capturing the flowers and making her heart stutter at the same time. "Let's put the rest in water, and take Fred and Ethel to the concert. They'll be our table decoration, even if our table is a blanket on the ground."

It was a beautiful day, warm, sunny, the kind of day that begged to be enjoyed. She thought of the things she had planned to do at home—laundry, vacuuming, dusting. Catching up with her life, essentially, after a long week of work. Not an ounce of that appealed to her right now, but the thought of spending time outside, with Fred and Ethel and Jack, did.

He's the enemy. The one who destroyed your father. Every time you see him, it will remind you of that history.

But was that really what had her hesitating? Or was

it what Jack had said, that she was afraid to go after the very things she helped her clients find?

"Come on, Marnie. Enjoy the day. Consider this your civic duty, supporting local high schools," he said, "albeit, civic duty accompanied by a glass of chardonnay."

"Oh, that sounds really good," she said, because it did, and because her resistance had been depleted when he'd named the daisy. She bit her lip, then shoved the doubts to the back of her mind. She wanted this afternoon, this moment. She pressed the Ethel daisy into his hand. "Hold these and I'll be back in two minutes. I have a vase in my office."

She ran back into the building, and up the stairs. In a few minutes, she had the daisies in some water, and had placed the vase by her desk, so she'd see them first thing every day. She was about to leave, then put a hand to her hair, and ducked into the restroom instead. She washed up, then placed her hands on either side of the sink and stared up at her reflection. Excitement and anticipation showed in her eyes, pinked in her cheeks.

Excitement and anticipation because she was going out with Jack Knight.

"What the hell are you doing?" she said to her image. "You can't get involved with him. He's all wrong for you, remember?"

Her image didn't reply. Nor did her brain rush forward with any reasons why Jack was wrong, exactly. For some reason, she couldn't come up with a single objection.

Even as she told herself she didn't care what Jack Knight thought about her appearance, she gave her hair a quick brush, then refastened the barrette holding the chestnut waves off her face. A quick swipe of blush, a little lipstick, then a quick exchange of heels for a pair of flats she kept under her desk. She grabbed a cardigan from the hook by the door, then, at the last second, she unclipped the barrette and dropped it on the counter. Her hair tumbled to her shoulders.

Unfettered, untamed.

His words came back to her, tempting, sexy, urging her to take a chance, to give him a chance. To just…be.

She stopped when she saw him standing by the silver car, holding Fred and Ethel. The last of her reservations melted away.

One day, one concert, wouldn't change anything. She'd have a good time, and be home before dark. Right?

CHAPTER EIGHT

WRONG.

The thick plaid blanket had seemed big when Marnie and Jack spread it on the grassy field that lay in front of the famous Hatch Shell. Hundreds of other families were camped out around them, armed with video cameras to capture their child's performance. The first band sat on the stage under the giant white dome, tuning their instruments while the A/V staff ran back and forth, doing last minute prep.

Marnie took a seat beside Jack and arranged her skirt over her knees and legs. She'd kicked off her shoes, left her cell phone in the car. Sitting in the sun, barefoot, with nowhere to go but right here, right now, had a decadent quality. For a while, the nagging thought that she should be doing something tensed in her shoulders. But as the sun washed its gentle warmth over her, Marnie began to relax, one degree at a time.

Well, relax as much as she could sitting next to Jack. He was so close that she caught the spicy dark notes of his cologne with every inhale. Her hand splayed on the blanket, inches from his. He had strong hands, the kind that looked like they could take care of her in one instant, and send her soaring to new heights in the bedroom in the next.

"Hungry?" Jack asked.

"Oh, yeah," she said, then colored when she realized that her hunger was for him, not food. Damn. What was with this man? Why did he draw her in so easily? She had already made that mistake with someone else. She straightened, putting a few centimeters of distance between them. "Uh, did you say you brought sandwiches?"

"Yep. Ham and cheese good with you?"

"Yes, thank you." She took one of the paper wrapped sandwiches from him and opened it. A thick pile of honey ham, topped with a generous portion of provolone cheese, as well as deep green Boston lettuce and juicy red tomato slices peeked out from between two rustic slices of sourdough bread. She took a bite, and goodness invaded her palate. "Oh, my. This is amazing. What's on this?"

"Hector's own jalapeno/cilantro mayonnaise. He owns the deli, and there are some meals that I think could get him nominated for sainthood."

Marnie took another bite. "Oh, this, definitely."

Jack chuckled, then uncorked the wine and poured it into two plastic cups, handing her one of them. "Plastic isn't exactly high brow, but I'm not exactly a fancy glass kind of guy."

"Really? You strike me as, well, as the opposite. Or at least, you have the other times I've run into you."

"It's those damned suits. They make me look all boring and dull."

She laughed. "Those are *not* the adjectives I'd use to describe you."

"Oh, really?" He arched a brow. "And how would you describe me?"

She thought a minute. "Mysterious. Guarded. An

enigma." That much was true. Every time she thought she had Jack figured out, he threw her a curveball.

"Ah, the elusive guy in the shadows who never opens his heart, is that it?" He raised his cup toward hers. "To guarded hearts."

"You talking about me?"

He laughed. "You, Marnie, have the most guarded heart I've ever seen."

"Touché." She gave him a nod of concession, then a smile. "To guarded hearts. And mysterious enigmas." They touched cups, then drank. Two kindred souls, in relationships at least.

"I don't think I ever thanked you for introducing my stepfather to your mom."

"I should be thanking you for encouraging him to go to the mixer. He really seems perfect for her." Marnie didn't think she'd ever seen her mother this happy, yet at the same time, the caution flags stayed in her head. Dan came with Jack—and could her mother handle that? "He's a nice guy."

Jack nodded. "He was a heck of a stepdad, too. He married my mom when I was eight, and was one of those hands-on dads. The kind that plays catch in the yard and teaches you how to build a fire with a flint and some kindling. But the years before Dan came along were…rough."

"I'm sorry." And she was. No child should have a difficult childhood. Hers hadn't been perfect, but it hadn't been rough, either.

Jack shrugged like it was no big deal, but she got the sense it did bother him. "My father was never there. Not then, not later."

"Did he work a lot?"

Jack snorted. "My father made work a world-class

sport. Heck, I saw the Tooth Fairy more than my own dad. And when he was home, his attention span lasted about five minutes before he was off on another call or writing another memo. Eventually, my mother had enough of being, essentially, a single mom, and divorced him."

"Yet you followed your father into the family business, from the day you graduated Suffolk." When he arched a brow in question, she gave Jack a little smile. "I Googled you."

"So you *are* interested in me?"

"Cautious. You never know who you're riding home with."

Jack laughed and tipped his cup of wine toward her. "True."

She picked off another tiny bite of ham. "So if you and your father had such a bad relationship, why did you go to work for him?"

Jack leaned an arm over his knee. His gaze went to somewhere in the distance, far from the performance at the Hatch Shell, far from her. "Even though I loved Dan, I never got past that need for a father's love and attention. Pretty pathetic, huh?"

"No, not at all." Another thread of connection knitted between them. Her father had worked countless hours as he built his business. She could relate to that craving for a relationship, a connection. She too had missed out on the camping trips and ball games with her father.

Her sympathy for Jack doubled. In his eyes, she could still see that hurting, hopeful boy, and it broke her heart.

Across from them, a mother and father took turns playing peek-a-boo with a baby in a stroller. The baby's laugh carried on the air, infectious, bubbly. That was what a family looked like, she thought, the kind of family Jack should have had his entire childhood, and it added a sad punctuation to their conversation.

Jack sighed. "Anyway, I guess I hoped that if I worked for him, we'd finally have that relationship I had missed out on."

She had wondered the same thing. If she had worked for her father, would she have had a closer relationship with him? Been able to help his business? Help him? "And did you get that relationship?"

"Oh, I saw him at work. When I was getting called into his office for another 'stupid' mistake. We didn't have long, father-son talks or take lunch together or even work on projects together. Everything I learned came from the other guys who worked for my father. Many of those men still work for me today, and they're almost like a second family."

"Why didn't you leave the company?" she asked.

"I did. Took a job at another business brokerage firm, and barely had time to put my pens in the drawer of my desk before I got a call telling me my father had had a heart attack. Two days later, I was in charge. After he died, I stepped into his shoes. Well, his office." A wry, sad grin crossed his face. "I made my own shoes."

She picked at an errant thread on the blanket, hating that they had this in common, too. Of all the people in Boston, why did she have to relate so closely to Jack, and his loss?

Jack's blue eyes met hers and his features softened. "I'm sorry, Marnie. I know your father died too, a few years ago. He was a heck of a nice guy, and I'm sure that loss was hard on you."

She heard true sympathy in Jack's voice and it made tears spring to her eyes. He covered her hand with his.

An easy, comfortable touch. One that eased the loss in her heart, yet at the same time it drove that pain home.

Damn him. Damn Jack for making her care. Damn Jack for caring about her. And damn Jack for being the reason behind all of this.

But he said he had quit, walked away. Then returned to do things his own way. Did that mean he had changed? That other businesses weren't being hurt like her father's? That her biggest argument against him was fizzling?

"I guess we never outgrow the need for a parent, huh?" he said.

She heard the echoes of her own loss in his voice, and it muddled the issues. She wanted to hate him—

And instead commiserated with Jack, this complex, layered man who had gone through so many of the same hurts as she had.

"Jack! Jack!" A blonde waved at them from a few feet away. A dark-haired man stood beside her, loaded down with a diaper bag, two lawn chairs and a small cooler.

Jack grinned, then got to his feet and put a hand out to Marnie. "Come on, let me introduce you to my cousin Ashley. She's the mom of the talented musician we're here to see."

"Oh, I don't think I should…" she said.

"I promise, they won't bite," he said, then took her hand and hauled her to her feet. So fast, she collided with his chest. He grinned and held her gaze for one long, hot moment. "Though I can't promise I won't."

A delicious thrill raced through her veins. Marnie released Jack's hand and bent down to straighten her skirt, and break that hypnotic connection. "Uh, maybe we should hurry because the concert's about to start." Anything to get some distance, some breathing room.

But then Jack took her hand again to help her as they picked their way among the lawn chairs and blankets and people on the lawn. He shifted his touch to the small of Marnie's back when they reached his cousin. "Hey, Ashley," he said. "This Marnie. Marnie, this is my cousin Ashley and her husband Joe."

"Nice to meet you," Ashley said, shaking hands with Marnie. Her husband echoed the sentiment, then nodded toward a little girl running across the back lawn.

"I'll be back. Have to go catch a runaway toddler." Joe lowered the things in his arms to the ground, then headed off at a light jog. Ashley unfolded the lawn chairs and placed them on either side of the cooler and diaper bag.

"I hear you have a talented son," Marnie said.

"Jack likes to brag about him, but yeah." Ashley's face lit with a mother's pride. "We think he's pretty amazing. And thank you, Jack, for making the time to be here."

"You know I'd never miss something like this."

"He'll be thrilled you came." Ashley gave Jack's hand a squeeze. "You're a great godfather." Then she turned to Marnie and grinned. "If the way he treats his godchildren is any indication, this one's going to be a great dad. Just in case you were wondering."

Marnie's face heated. "Oh, he and I, we're not… together."

"Pity," Ashley said. "Because I'd love to spoil Jack's kids rotten. Maybe even buy them a drum set for Christmas, like he did for our kids."

Jack chuckled. "Hey, that drum set led to him being on that stage."

"True. But next time, I'm letting my kids sleep over

at your house when they need to practice." Ashley laughed.

The warmth and love between the cousins mirrored the camaraderie Marnie had with her own family, and again showed another dimension to Jack Knight. A man who loved and was loved, not the man she'd vilified for years. Her resistance lowered even more.

The three of them talked for a little while longer, then Jack took Marnie's hand. "They're about to start," he said. "We better get back to our spot."

Joe returned with a tow-headed toddler in his arms. "She says she wants Uncle Jack."

The girl scrambled out of her father's arms and up into Jack's. "Uncle Jack, are you comin' to our house later? Mamma made cake."

"Cake, huh?" Jack beeped the girl's nose. "Is it as sweet as you?"

She nodded. "Uh-huh. It's chocolate. With bubber dream."

"Buttercream," Ashley corrected, moving to take her daughter and hand her a juice box. "Bad for the hips and the heart, but oh, so good."

Jack chuckled. "Sure. I'll stop by tonight. And I might just have a surprise if you're good."

The little girl straightened and nodded, as solemn as a judge. "Imma good girl."

"Of course you are," he said quietly. Then he ruffled her hair. "Okay, good girl, watch your brother. I'll see you later."

Marnie and Jack walked back over to their blanket, and took their seats again. "Your family was really nice," she said. And they were. She had liked them, a lot.

"Thanks. I never had any brothers or sisters, so my

cousins are like my siblings. Most of them still live in the area, and I see them pretty often. If I ever have a kid, I'm calling Ashley and Joe for advice." He sent a fond look in their direction.

"She's adorable."

"She's four. Smart as a whip, and a bottle full of sass, according to her mother, but yes, adorable."

Jack's face showed the soft spot in his heart for his cousin's children. For his family. It drew her in, even as she tried to keep distance between them. Marnie kept her hands away from his under the guise of eating, but really, it was because it had become far too easy and natural to connect with Jack. To let down that wall, to let herself…be.

To fall for him.

"How's your sandwich?" Jack asked.

She jerked her attention back to him. "Oh, uh, perfect." And it was. Low-key, easy, simple. Marnie found herself giving in to the relaxing day, the bucolic setting, the contentment of good food. Just the two of them—okay and three hundred other adults and kids—enjoying a lunch outdoors. The first band began to play, and both Jack and Marnie sat back and listened, while they ate their sandwiches and sipped the wine. As the first song edged into the second, then the third, she started to truly enjoy herself. Maybe it was the sunshine. The food in her belly. The wine. But by the time the second band came on the stage, Marnie was leaning on her elbows, with Jack so close, she could feel his shoulder brush hers every once in a while. She didn't move away. She wasn't sure she could if she wanted to.

"This is my cousin's school coming on stage now," he said, turning to speak to her.

She pivoted at the same time, which brought their

mouths within kissing distance. Heat ignited in the space between them, and her gaze dropped to his mouth. Anticipation pooled in her gut.

The band launched into an up-tempo jazz selection. Marnie jerked back, clasped her hands in her lap and concentrated on the music. Not on almost kissing Jack.

The quartet played plucky notes accented by a soft touch on the drums, and occasional taps of the high hat. It was a simple group, with drums, a bass, a sax, and a piano. The players would look up from time to time, grin at one another, and then play through a complex section of the music. The last few notes tapered off and applause began to swell.

"They were terrific," Marnie said over the sound of their clapping hands. "Which one is your cousin?"

"The pianist." Pride beamed in Jack's features. "He's a great kid. Really talented. He's applied at Berklee, and he has a great chance of getting in."

"I can see why." She sat back as the band exited the stage, and made room for the next one. "I wish I had even an ounce of their musical ability. I couldn't carry a tune if you taped one to my mouth."

He chuckled. "Oh, I don't know about that. You have such a pretty voice, I bet you can sing."

She put up her hands to ward off the possibility, but the compliment warmed her. "My sister Kat, who became a graphic designer, got all the creative genes in the family."

"I think matchmaking is pretty creative, don't you?"

"True." She leaned her head on her shoulder and studied him. "What about you? Any creativity in those genes?"

He grinned. "Depends on what kind of creativity you're looking for."

Her face heated—God, what was it with this man, turning her face red all the time—as she realized the double entendre. "I meant the ones in your DNA, not the bedroom kind."

"I know." He leaned over and ran a finger over her cheek. Her pulse skittered. "I just like to see you blush."

Oh, my. This man hit all the right buttons, and as much as part of her cursed him for doing it, another part liked it. Very much. She'd dated men, but none had knocked her so off-kilter, leaving her breathless, distracted, *wanting.*

When he looked at her, she felt beautiful. When he smiled like that, she felt sexy. And when his voice lowered like that, it set off a chain reaction of desire deep, deep inside her body.

She jerked around to a sitting position, drawing her knees up to her chest. "Oh, look, the next band is on stage."

Was she that desperate for a man in her life that she'd fall for the one man who had helped ruin her father?

Or that scared of falling for someone who turned her world so inside-out? Being with Jack was like racing down a track on the back of a runaway car. And that was the one thing that made Marnie want to bolt.

A few minutes later, the concert was over, and the attendees began gathering up blankets and lawn chairs, and start trekking back across the grassy lawn to their cars. The skies had begun to darken, and in the distance, Marnie heard the low rumble of thunder. "We better hurry," she said, "before we get caught in the storm."

But even as she bundled up the blanket and helped gather the remnants of their lunch, Marnie had a feeling she'd already gotten caught by a storm. One made by Jack Knight.

* * *

They didn't move fast enough.

A second later, the thick gray clouds broke open with an angry burst of wind and water, dropping rain in fast sheets over the Esplanade and the hundreds of people scrambling for their cars. Jack grabbed Marnie's hand. "Come on, let's go!"

They charged across the grass, weaving through the other people, as the rain fell. Finally, they reached the car, and collapsed against it in a tangle of arms, legs and picnic supplies. "Wait!" she said. "I dropped the blanket."

"Don't worry about it. I'll get another." He fumbled in his pocket for the keys, then unlocked Marnie's door. A second later, they were both safe inside the dry car. He took the picnic supplies from her and tossed everything onto the back seat. The leather seats would probably end up ruined, but right now, Jack didn't care.

Even with the rain, the day had been one of the best he could remember having. All his life, he'd sucked at personal relationships, putting the people in his life on the sidelines while he concentrated on work. He'd worried that he'd be his father's son with women, too, that he would leave a trail of broken hearts to match the trail of broken companies.

No more.

For the first time in forever, Jack wanted to try harder, to be better, for himself and with others. He didn't want to just give back to companies, or connect with business owners, or repay those his father had hurt, he wanted to do the same turnaround with himself. He used to think that if he could just make amends for his father's choices, he would be complete. But now he wanted more.

He wanted everything his father had never appreciated. The white picket fence, the two kids, the dog in the yard. The woman who greeted him with a smile at the end of the day.

Marnie had brought that out in him. She was a challenge, a puzzle, one he wanted to solve. He had a feeling this complex, beautiful woman would keep him on his toes for a really, really long time. And oh, how he craved that.

Craved *her.*

Marnie shook her head, then swiped off the worst of the rain. Even soaking wet, she looked amazing. Water had darkened her lashes, plastered her hair to her head, and soaked the pale yellow shirt she wore, until it outlined every delicious inch of her torso. She leaned down and plucked at her skirt. "God, I'm soaked. Maybe we should hit a Laundromat and throw ourselves into a dryer." She glanced up, and caught him looking at her. "What?"

Desire pulsed in his veins, pounded in his heart. Coupled with the darkened interior of the car, the intimacy of the black leather seats, and the rain drumming a steady beat on the roof, it seemed as if they were the only two people in the world.

"You're soaking wet," he said.

She laughed. "I know. I said that."

"And still one of the most beautiful women I have ever seen in my life." That caused another blush to fill her cheeks. Damn, he liked that about her. A touch of vulnerable, mixed in with the strong. He reached out, brushed a lock of hair off her cheek. It left a little glistening trail of water, and before he could think better of it, he leaned across the console and kissed that line, kissed all the way down her cheek, until he moved a few millimeters to the left and caught her lips with his.

"We...shouldn't do this," Marnie whispered against his mouth.

"Okay," he said, then kissed her again. She tasted of wine and vanilla and all he wanted right now was more, more, and even more of her. He slid one hand up, along the smooth side of her blouse, then around the curve of her breast. The thin, wet fabric offered almost no barrier against the lace edges of her bra, the stiff peak of her nipple.

When his fingers danced over it, Marnie gasped and arched forward. *"Jack."*

He'd heard his name a million times in his life. Never had that single syllable sounded so sweet. He opened his mouth against hers, and with a groan, deepened the kiss, shifting to capture more of her breast, more of her, more of everything.

Her hands came up around his back, clutching at him, nearly dragging him over the console. Her kiss turned wild, ferocious, and that sent him into a dizzying tailspin of want, need. The rain pounded harder, thunder booming above them, lightning crackling in the sky, as the storm between them became a wild ride of hands and tongues.

His fingers went to the buttons on her blouse, then stilled when he heard a horn honk, the rev of an engine. Damn. They were still in the parking lot, surrounded by other people. "We should take this somewhere more private," he said. His breath heaved in and out of his chest.

She drew back, her lips red and swollen, her breath also coming in little fast gasps. Her green eyes met his, held, then her breathing slowed. She shook her head. "How do you do that?"

"Do what?"

"Get me to forget all the very good reasons I have for not letting you get close. We can't do this, Jack. Not now, not ever. It's...wrong."

"It sure felt right. And explosive. And crazy, and a hundred other things."

She sighed. "That's the problem."

The rain began to slow, one of those fast-moving storms that passed almost as fast as it started. The parking lot cleared out, families going home to dinners in the oven, homework at the kitchen table. He put his hand on the ignition but didn't turn the key. "Then why did you kiss me?"

She bit her lip. "Because, for a little while, I forgot. And just...was."

"Forgot what?"

But Marnie just shook her head and asked him to drive her home. He started the car, pulled out of the lot, and headed southwest. But as he watched the Hatch Shell get smaller and smaller in his rearview mirror, Jack had a feeling he'd lost more than just a blanket today.

CHAPTER NINE

JACK HAD RUINED HER.

Ever since the walk to the neighborhood coffee shop and the jazz concert on the lawn, she'd found her office too confining. She'd spent more time outside in the last few days than she had all year, and as the morning wore on and the sun made its journey across the sky, Marnie got more and more antsy. She paced. She hummed. She fiddled. In short, she didn't do a damned thing productive.

Erica got to her feet, and grabbed Marnie's car keys. "Okay, that's it. I'm tired of you bouncing in place. Let's get out of here and go grab something to eat. Preferably something chocolate and really, really bad for us."

"But I've got all this work—"

"To do tomorrow. It can wait, especially considering you haven't done much of it so far today." Erica arched a brow, then grinned.

"Why are you smiling about that?" Marnie ran a hand through her hair and let out a sigh. "All it does is put me further behind. I have this long list of clients waiting for me to find them a match. All these events to organize and—"

"Step out of your comfort zone, Marn, and blow off work today. There are days when you are wound tighter than a ball of yarn, which is pretty much par for the course with you, oh, control freak sister. But these last couple weeks…" Erica shrugged.

"What?"

"These last couple weeks, you've been smiling and laughing, and…" Erica put a hand on her sister's and met Marnie's gaze. "Well, it's been nice."

Marnie refused to give Jack Knight any credit for the change in her attitude. If anything, he'd made things worse, not better. Except…

The walk through the quaint neighborhood and the jazz concert at the Hatch Shell had been fun. Even running in the rain had left her breathless, laughing. It had all been a huge step out of her comfort zone and oddly, she'd enjoyed it. What had he said to her the other day?

You should let your hair down more often.

Right or wrong, Jack Knight had gotten her to do exactly that in the last couple weeks. She'd slept better at night, worked better during the day, and the tension had eased in her shoulders. Maybe Jack had a point. She hated that he did, but he did.

"So…who is he?" Erica asked.

"Who's who?"

"The man who has you all atwitter. You're like a girl in junior high." Erica pointed at her sister. "There, that. You're blushing. You *never* blush."

Marnie sighed. "He's Jack Knight. The owner of Knight Enterprises."

A light dawned in Erica's eyes and she let out a little gasp. "Jack *Knight?* Of Knight Enterprises infamy? The same one that invested in Dad's business years ago?"

Marnie nodded, then explained how she'd met Jack, and what had transpired in the weeks since, leaving off the bit about kissing him.

"Okay, but that still doesn't explain why you blush every time you talk about him," Erica said.

Marnie sighed. "He kissed me."

"He...*what?* He *kissed* you? Really? Oh, my God," she said, her voice reaching Roberta-worthy decibels. "Did you kiss him back?"

"Yes, but only because he took me by surprise. And it won't happen again, I can tell you that. I reacted out of...instinct."

Yeah, right. She'd kissed him because of a reflex, not desire. *Liar.*

Erica typed something into the laptop computer beside her, waited a second, then turned the screen toward Marnie. "Oh, I'm sure it was instinct to kiss *that* hunk of yummy. Any woman with a pulse's instinct."

Marnie looked at Jack's image, one of those professional photos done for the corporate website. He had a serious, no-nonsense look on his face, along with a navy power suit and a dark crimson tie. The Jack Knight in the photo was powerful, commanding. None of the teasing looks or charming grins he'd given her. And yet, her body reacted the same, with that instant zing of desire. Curse the man for being so damned good looking. "Okay, so he's cute."

"So, what are you going to do about him? Now that you're done kissing him?"

"I don't know. I want to hate him, and I do, I really do, but..."

"A part of you is starting to like him?"

Marnie shook her head. "No, not at all."

Erica just laughed. "You do realize that when you shook your head, you then gave a slight nod? If this were an interrogation, it would totally negate your strong protests to the contrary."

"The trouble is, he seems nice. Not at all the evil corporate raider I pictured." Marnie thought of the gym he'd invested in, the coffee shop owner who loved him and raved about him, the family he adored. Twice, Jack had told her he wasn't as bad as she thought he was, yet he represented everything that had hurt her mother, her family. She shook her head. "Either way, he's all wrong for me."

"Then you better stop kissing him," Erica said with a grin. "Or next you'll end up in bed with the enemy."

Later that morning, Marnie and Erica closed up the office and headed across town to the Second Chance shelter and work counseling center. The two of them had been volunteering there for years, a good cause that helped struggling people find work.

Even though her workload had quadrupled because of the distracting thoughts about Jack, Marnie welcomed the break from the office. She'd get away from her sister's prying eyes, the ringing of the telephone, and the daisies that still sat on her desk. All reminders of Jack, and how close she kept coming to falling for Mr. Wrong.

She wanted a steady, dependable man. One who wanted a quiet, predictable life. None of this heady, crazy, spontaneity that came with Jack. He was a risk, a giant one. Hadn't she already seen how bad a risk like that could ruin someone? She had no desire to do the same.

A silver sports car glided to a stop in the lane beside her, and she flicked a quick glance at the driver. Darn it. Every silver car she saw reminded her of Jack Knight. Heck, even though she knew better, he'd been on her mind the better part of the day and nearly all night. Her hormones hadn't gotten the memo from her brain that he was No Good for Her. Maybe she just needed more time.

And less silver sports cars on the Boston roads. Because despite her better judgment, she couldn't stop from looking in the driver's side window, a part of her hoping to see a dark-haired, blue-eyed man.

Erica had dropped the subject of Jack, thank goodness, and talked on the drive about her plans for the weekend. They drove across town, then parked outside a converted two-family home that had been turned into a combination shelter and education center for people down on their luck. Second Chance had been started a few years ago by a group of local businesspeople who wanted to give back to the community, and had been successful with a large percentage of the people it served. Marnie had supported the organization from day one with monetary donations, a couple of career workshops, and clothing donations. She'd used her network to help several of the residents find jobs, and sent numerous leads to the director. It was a good cause, and one she wished every business in Boston would get behind.

She and Erica grabbed two big bags of clothes Marnie had to donate, and headed inside. Linda, the director, came out of her office to help. Linda was a tall, thin, energetic woman who always had a ready smile for everyone she met. Her ash blond hair was pulled back in a ponytail, which gave her blue floral dress and practical white sneakers a fun touch. "Oh, bless you, Marnie. The ladies here will be so glad to see all this."

"No problem. It's the least I can do. Where do you want everything?"

Linda directed her to a room down the hall that had

been converted into a giant closet. "Marnie, if you could just set the items up on the hangers, then they'll be ready for after our event. Oh, and Erica, since you're here, too, can I borrow you to help with lunch service for a little bit? We're short-handed today. We had more people than I expected show up to hear our speaker today."

"Sure. I'd be glad to." Erica headed into the kitchen, while Marnie hung up the clothes and set up the shoes she'd brought. It was good, easy, mindless work that kept her from dwelling on impossible situations.

Ten minutes later, Marnie had finished. The antsy feeling had yet to go away, so she started straightening and pacing again. From down the hall, she heard a strong round of applause and the murmur of voices.

The speaker Linda had mentioned. Whoever it was, he or she was enjoying an enthusiastic response from the attendees. Linda often brought in motivational speakers, who left their listeners with a renewed enthusiasm. Might be worth popping in for a minute and listening, Marnie decided. It was better than rehanging shirts and straightening skirts, or wearing a path from the hall to the window.

She crossed into a large room that used to be a dining room, but had been opened up and turned into a mini auditorium, now utilized for speakers, AA meetings, and other events. Rows and rows of folding chairs filled the space, and not a one was vacant. At the podium stood a tall, thin man Marnie recognized as Harvey, a frequent visitor to Second Chance. He had started out homeless, addicted to drugs, and had turned his life around in recent years, becoming a volunteer and counselor at the very place that helped him. She liked

Harvey, especially his positive attitude and his belief in perseverance.

"I can't thank this man enough for what he did," Harvey was saying. "He gave me a job when no one else would, he told me he believed in me when no one else did, and he became a friend when no one else was around. I'm proud as heck to introduce my mentor and good friend, Jack Knight, to all of you."

Marnie bit back a gasp. Jack? Here? Being touted as the best thing to come along since sliced bread? By Harvey of all people?

She ducked to the right to hide behind a thick green potted plant, just as Jack strode into the room, wearing jeans and a pale green button-down shirt that made his eyes seem even bluer. Her body reacted with a rush of heat, and her mind replayed that kiss in the car. God, she wanted him, even now, even when she shouldn't.

He stepped up to the podium, thanking Harvey for his warm introduction. The crowd greeted Jack with renewed enthusiasm, and several shouted his name and a welcome back. After the applause died down, Jack began to speak.

She expected one of those speeches about corporate responsibility. Or putting your best foot forward in a job interview. But instead, Jack delivered a commentary that had the audience riveted, and Marnie rooted to the spot.

"You will always have people who will tell you that your dreams aren't worth having," Jack said. "People who think their way is the only way, and that anyone who takes another path is wrong. They'll try to cut you down, or talk you out of your plans. Work to convince you that they have the right answers, or maybe even tell you to pull the plug and give up. Move on. Do something else. It can take a great deal of courage to forge forward, to keep believing in yourself. But I'm here to tell you that it's worth it in the end."

Applause, a few whoops of support.

Jack nodded, then went on. He didn't read from cue cards, or anything prepared, but rather, seemed to speak from his heart. His gaze connected with every person in the audience, and they connected right back with him. "You've heard the old adage that you have to fight for what you believe in, and that is true. But they don't tell you that the first fight you have to have is for yourself. Start by fighting for you, and fighting those doubts that keep you stuck in the wrong place, because *you* matter." At this, he pointed at the crowd, then at Harvey, then at himself. "And once you know that, the rest of the battle gets easier."

More applause, more whoops. Marnie felt a hand on her shoulder and turned to find Erica beside her.

"Oh, my God, is that Jack Knight?" Erica asked.

Marnie nodded. "I had no idea he was going to be here today."

"Wow, he's even cuter in person than he is in his picture," Erica whispered. "And without the suit and tie, he's downright sexy."

"He is," Marnie admitted. "And the people here love him. His speech is great."

"Seems to me that's a good enough reason to take a chance on him." Erica shrugged. "We could have him all wrong."

"Or he could be the greatest BS artist to come along in years."

"True. But he did bring you daisies. Doesn't that mean he deserves a second look? Or at least a chance to explain why he did what he did with Dad's business?" Erica cast another glance at Jack. "Until you do, I don't think you can truly know whether to hate him or love him."

"Love him?" Marnie scoffed. "I can barely stand him."

Erica laughed. "Oh, yeah, I can see that in the way you stare at him."

"I fixed him up with other women, Erica. I'm not interested in Jack Knight."

Except she had gone out on two, no, three dates with him, if she counted the dinner with their parents. And she'd been thinking about him non-stop for days. Kissed him twice. Desired him more than she'd desired anyone else.

"Pity. He seems like a really nice guy." Erica glanced over her shoulder, saw Linda heading for the kitchen and gave her sister a light touch on the shoulder. "I have to get back to lunch service. Just remember what Dad used to say. You can't judge the house until you see the inside. You don't know the whole story of Dad's house, and you don't know the whole story of Jack's. You don't know if Jack tried to help Dad and he refused to listen. Our father was a great visionary but not the best businessman in the world."

"All the more reason why he needed an investor who would help him, not just throw some money at him then step back and watch him drown. Regardless, Jack is a constant reminder to all of us of what happened with Dad. We don't need that in our lives."

"Maybe. But you won't know unless *you ask him about it.*" Erica leaned in to whisper in Marnie's ear, with emphasis on the last few words. "Stop being afraid to look inside and find out the truth. You keep this tight little leash on everything, Marnie. Sometimes taking a risk is good for you, and your heart."

Erica left the room. Marnie debated following, but Jack's voice drew her in again. "That's the business I'm really in," he was saying, "one where I support dreams. I am honored to have been rewarded for my work, too."

Financially, the cynic in Marnie thought.

"I'm not talking about money," Jack said as if he'd read her mind. "It's the people. When you put passion and belief into what you do, it translates into the people around you, and you pay it forward with every business decision you make. For me, it's the bookstore owner who has the funds to start a literacy program for adult learners. The daycare owner who can now afford to offer a drop-in service for parents who are looking for jobs. The handyman firm that has expanded into two more cities, and hired great people like Harvey here. These are people who took a risk and it paid off. Their thank-yous are worth more than any number on the bottom line, and at the end of the day, bring you a satisfaction you won't find anywhere else." He stepped out from behind the podium and into the audience, as far as the mike's cord allowed. "So take a chance, go after your dreams, and you'll enjoy a return on that investment that is ten-fold."

The audience erupted into applause. People got to their feet, cheering Jack and his words, reaching for him to tell him how impressed they were, thanking him for his message.

Heck of a speech, Marnie thought. Almost had her convinced he was a nice guy.

The crowd began to disperse, some people heading for the platters of cookies and coffee at the back of the room, while others opted for lunch in the kitchen. Many of the people raved about Jack's speech, clear fans of him now. Maybe her father had been sold on some "support the dream" speech, too, and been too blind to see the reality of the situation.

Except that didn't match the father she'd known. Yes, he'd been terrible at business—more of a creative than an accountant—but he'd been an incredible judge of character. Tom could pick a con artist out of a room of a hundred people, and many of the people he'd had handshake deals with over the years had turned out to be his best friends. He'd known in a minute if someone had a good heart or bad intentions.

If that was so, then why had he signed an agreement with Knight Enterprises? How could he have missed the writing on the wall? Or had Jack tried, and failed, to help Tom's business?

He brought you daisies, Erica had said. *Doesn't that mean he deserves a second look?*

Marnie lingered in the room, watching Jack interact with several of the people at Second Chance. She stayed behind her veil of greenery, her feet rooted to the spot. A woman Marnie knew well, a single mom named Luanne, stepped over to Jack. Within seconds, Luanne was crying, and Marnie's heart went out to her. She knew life had been tough for Luanne lately—not only had she lost her job, but also her home after a bitter divorce. She'd been staying at Second Chance for a few weeks now and had been the one with the idea of a donated career dress day to help the women looking for work.

"You told us to follow our dreams," Luanne said to Jack, "but I lost all mine. I don't know what to do now."

Jack's face was kind, his eyes soft. "What did you do before for work?"

"Data entry at a newspaper, working in the subscription department."

"And did you love that?"

The room had emptied out, with most of the people heading for lunch in the kitchen, a few lingering in the hall. Spring sunshine streamed in through the windows, bright, cheery, hopeful, like it was trying to coax Luanne into believing brighter days were on the horizon.

Luanne shook her head. "I hated that job. I only took it because I wanted to be a writer. Then one year turned into two, turned into ten…" She shrugged.

Jack reached into his breast pocket and pulled out a pen, one of those expensive ones, with a heavy silver barrel. He pressed the ballpoint into the woman's hand. "Take this," he said, "and write with it."

"Write what?"

"About your journey. About your life lessons. About anything you want. Back when I was young and had lots to say, I wrote novels and short stories. I even started out in college pursuing a degree in writing, before I switched to a major in business. A part of me still loves writing, the whole process of collecting my thoughts and forming them into stories." Jack shrugged. "No one will ever read what I write, but that's okay because it's just a hobby for me. You, though, you have a dream and a passion. I could see it in your eyes when I gave you the pen and said 'write.' It was as if that lit a fire deep inside you. So go, and write. The world needs more writers, especially ones with life experiences to share."

Luanne scoffed. "Who wants to hear my sob story?"

Jack held her gaze, and that smile Marnie had memorized curved across his face. "I do. And I bet the publisher at the community magazine wants to hear it, too. Send it my way when you're done, and I'll get it to him."

Tears glimmered in Luanne's eyes. She clutched the pen so tight, her knuckles whitened. "Thank you. Thank you so much."

"Don't thank me. Just take this dream, and spread it to another. Someday, you'll give someone else a pen or a kind word or some advice, and that will start them on their journey." Jack gave Luanne a gentle hug, then said goodbye and crossed to the coffeepot.

Marnie told her feet to move. Told herself to leave the room. But she remained cemented where she was, behind the plant, watching Jack approach.

Jack Knight, the demon who had destroyed her father, helping a woman down on her luck. Jack Knight, the man who kept getting her to step out of her comfort zone and let her hair down. Jack Knight, the man who had ignited something raw, urgent, and terrifying, deep inside her. Telling people to go after their dreams. Was it all a front?

A riot of emotions ran through her in the few seconds it took Jack to go from one end of the room to the other. She kept trying so hard to hate him but the feeling refused to stick.

In the end, indecision won out. Jack's blue eyes lit and his smile broadened when he spied her behind the plant. A sweet, delicious warmth spread through Marnie, and despite her better judgment, she found herself stepping out from behind the plant and giving him a smile of her own.

"Marnie."

When he said her name in that soft, surprised way, she was back in the car, the rain pounding on the roof, kissing Jack and thinking of nothing more than how much she wanted him, how he seemed to know every inch of her body so well. "I, uh, heard you talking and came in to listen. You gave a great speech."

"Thanks. I hope it touched a few people."

"It touched Luanne," she said, nodding in the direction the other woman had gone. Luanne had left the room with a lightness in her steps, a hopeful smile on her face, a changed woman. "That was really nice, what you did for her."

Jack shrugged. "It was a small thing."

"Not to Luanne. She's been through a lot, with her ex, and losing her job. I can tell that really touched her, to have someone believe in her." Marnie had to admit, that for all the bad Jack had done in the past, this moment would make a difference. She could already see a renewed enthusiasm and optimism in Luanne's features as she talked to other people in the room, showing off the pen, and spreading the words of encouragement.

"And yet, you run away every time I get close. You give me a laundry list of reasons why we shouldn't date." He took a step closer. "Why?"

She shook her head. "Jack, there's too much between us to make this work. Please stop trying to pretend there isn't."

He took another step closer, and the fronds of the plant brushed against his shoulder. "I'm not trying to pretend there isn't. But I'm willing to take the risk that we have something amazing here, something that is stronger than the past. The question is why you don't think so, too. Why you won't take a risk."

"I'm not interested in you. Or a relationship." But even as she said the words, Marnie knew, deep down inside, that they were a lie. She wanted all of that, and she wanted him—

But her wants couldn't overpower the tight hold she had on her life. If she let him in, if she took a chance—

No. She didn't do that. She didn't go off on haphazard paths, with no clear sense of direction. And that's what being with Jack was like. Insane and delicious, all at the same time. The whole thing made her want to hyperventilate.

"You make me want to take the day off, head for the Common with a bottle of wine and a picnic lunch," Jack said, his blue eyes capturing hers. "Or get in the car and drive up the coastline until we get to the tip of Maine, the edge of the country. Or just sit in a car while the rain falls and watch the way your eyes light up when I move closer and—"

She jerked away. How did he keep doing that? Every time she turned around, Jack wrapped her in his spell. Was that what he had done with her father, too? Spoken pretty words that masked Jack's true intentions? One Franklin had already fallen for Jack's words, had believed him when he'd offered a risky proposition. She refused to be the second one. "I have to go. I'm supposed to be helping my sister in the kitchen."

Then she spun on her heel and got out of the room, before temptation got the better of her. Although a part of Marnie suspected it already had.

CHAPTER TEN

JACK SAT AT his father's desk, in the office his father had spent most of his life in, and wished he could have a second chance, the very thing he'd promoted in his speech the other day. He'd told others they were possible, and had yet to find one in his own life, no matter how many hours he spent here. There were still things from the past catching up with him, nipping at his heels, and reminding him every day that he was his father's son—

And not at all proud of that fact.

The guilt of what he had done, the companies he had destroyed, the people whose hearts he had broken, gnawed at him still. The work he'd done over the last two years hadn't filled that aching hole in his heart the way he'd thought it would. It was as if he was sitting in the wrong chair, making the wrong choices. Impossible. He knew this was the right thing to do. But as he reached the end of the pile of folders, he had to wonder if that was true.

He'd told the people in that room to take a risk, to go after what they wanted. Had he taken his own advice?

He'd pursued Marnie, yes, but he'd also let her go. If he truly wanted her, what the hell was he doing here?

His assistant dropped off a stack of checks for Jack to sign. He thanked her, then began to scrawl his name across the bottom line. Each one he signed represented a new start for someone, a new chance. And another chance for Jack to make amends.

He paused on the last one. Doug Hendrickson's seed money. Jack held the check for a long time, then reached in his drawer, pulled out one of the dozens of keys stored in a box, and headed out of the office. As he left, he paused by his assistant's desk. "Cancel the rest of my appointments for today. And can you make sure this—" he grabbed a piece of paper and an envelope, then jotted a quick note on the white linen stock "—gets delivered immediately?"

"Sure," she said, then looked up at him. "If you don't mind my saying so, you look a little worried today. Everything okay?"

Jack glanced down at the note, then at the key in his hand. "Not yet. But I hope it will be."

Marnie returned from lunch, expecting the office to be empty. Erica had a doctor's appointment, and Marnie's schedule was clear for the rest of the day. But as she got out of her car, she saw a familiar car parked in Erica's spot, and her mother standing on the stoop. "Ma, what a nice surprise!"

Her mother held up a bag of cookies from a local bakery. "And I brought dessert."

"My favorite. And such a decadent treat after I just had a salad." Marnie unlocked the office door and waved her mother inside. "Let me put on some coffee."

Marnie started the pot brewing, then got them two cups and a plate for the cookies, and set it all up in the reception area. "Thanks for bringing these. This is definitely a chocolate kind of day."

Her mother laughed. "I think that goes for every day."

"True, very true." Marnie grinned, then took a bite of a chocolate peanut butter cup cookie. Heaven melted against her palate. "These are…amazing."

Marnie and her mother ate, drank and chatted for a few minutes, catching up on family gossip. The cookies eased the tension lingering in Marnie's shoulders, a tension brought about by too many late-night thoughts about Jack, and their conversation at Second Chance yesterday.

I'm willing to take the risk that we have something amazing here, something that is stronger than the past. The question is why you don't think so, too. Why you won't take a risk.

Trust and fall. Just the thought caused Marnie's chest to tighten. She reached for another cookie and pushed the thoughts of Jack to the back of her mind. Stubborn, they refused to stay there, and lingered at the edge of her every word.

"Aren't you leaving tonight?" Marnie asked her mother. "For your big weekend in Maine?"

"About that…" Helen toyed with her coffee mug. "I'm not sure I should go."

"What? Why?"

"Because you're not okay with us being together, and the last thing I want to do is make you unhappy. You and your sisters are my world, Marnie." Ma's hand covered hers. Her pale green eyes met Marnie's. "I don't want to see you hurting."

"Ma, you were happy with Dan. He was happy with you. You deserve that."

A small, sad smile crossed Ma's face. "Not at the expense of your happiness."

In that instant, Marnie saw what her actions had cost. Not just herself, but those she loved. Her mother had given up the man she cared about—her second chance at love—to avoid hurting her daughter. Because Marnie had yet to be able to get over the past. She kept wanting to make Jack, and anyone associated with Jack, pay for something that had happened three years ago. Her mother had gotten past it, had moved on and started her life over. Marnie needed to do the same. "Here you are, protecting me, when I was trying to protect you." Marnie shook her head.

"Protect me? From what?"

"From being hurt. I thought if I didn't date Jack and you avoided Dan, that you wouldn't see Jack and think about what happened to Dad. But it's clear Dan makes you happy and that this isn't about the past anymore. It's about your future."

"Oh, honey—"

Marnie gave her mother's hand a squeeze. "You took a risk, and fell in love again—"

"Well, it's probably too soon to say fell in love." But the blush in Ma's cheeks belied that statement.

"And I think that's pretty incredible. Because..." Marnie drew back her hand and dropped her gaze to the cookies. Cookies that hadn't erased the issues, just muted them for a few bites. "Because I've been too terrified to do that myself."

There was the truth. Marnie didn't date because she was terrified of falling in love. It was the one emotion that meant giving up control, letting go. Trusting the other person would catch you.

Ma's face softened. "Marnie, don't let fear keep you from love. Or from Jack."

"I'm not talking about Jack." Or thinking about him.

Or dwelling on him. Except she was, all the time. And wondering if she took a risk on love with him, if she'd find the same happiness her mother had.

I'm willing to take the risk that we have something amazing here, something that is stronger than the past.

She realized she'd become the same thing she saw in her clients all the time, a gun-shy single who wanted love, but did everything she could to avoid a relationship. The matchmaker was terrified of matching herself.

How ironic.

"Jack's a good man, Marnie," Ma said as if reading her daughter's mind, "despite what he did in the past. He's changed, Dan said. Doing business in an entirely new way." Her mother's cell phone lit with an incoming call from Dan. A smile stole across Helen's face. The kind of smile of a woman in love, a woman who had found a man who loved her, too. A gift, Marnie realized, that not everyone found.

"Dan's a good man, too," Marnie said. She picked up the phone and placed it in her mother's palm, closing Ma's fingers over the slim silver body. "Tell him you'll go to Maine with him."

Ma hesitated. "Really?"

Marnie nodded. "He makes you smile, Ma, and that's all that's ever mattered to me."

The smile widened on Ma's face, and her eyes lit with joy. She pressed the button on her phone, and answered the call. Within seconds, Ma was giggling like a schoolgirl, and making plans with Dan. "Okay, sounds good," she said. "I'm looking forward to it, too. See you soon, Dan." Then she said goodbye and tucked the phone back into her purse.

Ma got to her feet and leaned over to give her daughter a warm hug. "You're a good daughter," she whispered, then she drew back and met her daughter's gaze with older, wiser, loving eyes. "Now take your own advice and take a chance on the man who makes you smile, too. A man like Jack, perhaps?"

"I don't know." Marnie hesitated. Jack distracted her, set her off her keel. That couldn't be a good thing, could it?

"If I were you," Ma said, "I'd make a list, just like you make your clients do. Figure out what's most important to you in the man you meet. And then use that instinct of yours to point you in the direction of Mr. Right."

Marnie shook her head. "I don't think it works on me. Too close to the work and all that."

"That's because you haven't tried." Ma wagged a finger at her. "And you never know what awaits around the next bend unless you travel down the road."

CHAPTER ELEVEN

AFTER THE COOKIE and coffee and chat with her mother, Marnie got back to work, instead of acting on her promised resolve to let Jack into her life. Erica returned from her appointment, and paused to hang up her coat, then stow her purse in the closet. When she got to her desk, she glanced across the room at her older sister. "Hey! Are those cookies on your desk?"

Marnie chuckled, and slid the plate in Erica's direction. "Ma stopped by with gifts."

"I thought she'd be halfway to Maine by now."

"She is now. She and I talked about Dan, and I'm cool with them dating. Ma is so happy, and it's nice to see. She deserves it."

Erica nodded. "It sure is. And if her being happy means we get cookies for lunch, then by all means, keep Dan around. Oh, I almost forgot!" Erica jumped up and dashed over to her desk, returning a second later with an envelope. "This came for you today when I was coming in the door. Delivered by messenger, so it must be important." She glanced at her watch. "Okay, I really gotta scoot. I'm supposed to meet with the caterer for our next event. Then I've got a date. You gonna be okay here without my astounding help?"

"Of course." Marnie tapped the envelope on her desk.

Plain, nondescript, nothing more than Marnie's name and address on the front. Probably a thank you from a satisfied client. "Thanks, Erica. Have fun on your date."

Erica's smile winged across her face. "You know me, I always do. And don't forget to have some fun yourself."

Marnie just nodded, then got back to work when Erica left. After a while, she stretched, and noticed the envelope again on the corner of her desk. She undid the flap, then pulled out the card inside.

I found something of your dad's at his shop that I think you're going to want to have. Your key should still work.
Jack

Marnie held on to the card for a long, long time. She turned it over, weighing her options. In the end, curiosity won, driven by the urge to see Jack again. Ever since the conversation with her mother, her thoughts had drifted toward the what-ifs. What if she fell for Jack? What if she kissed him again? What if they took things to the next level? Would she be going around with that same goofy, blissful smile on her face?

The card had been the impetus she needed, like a sign from above that she needed to stop dithering and start acting. Wasn't it about time she found out, instead of sitting on the sidelines, giving everyone else the happy ending she wanted, too? She grabbed her keys and headed across town, her heart in her throat.

In her mind, she kept seeing the four letters of *Jack.* Not *Love, Jack,* or *Thinking of you, Jack* or even *Best Wishes, Jack.* Just *Jack.* She should have been glad he'd left the closing impersonal, business-like. But she wasn't. She wanted more. She wanted him to come right out and say what he was feeling, and then let them take it from there. Even that thought made her heart beat a little faster with anxiety.

God, she really was a mess. But as she got closer to the building, and to seeing Jack, a smile spread across her face and anticipation warmed her veins. She thought of that kiss in the car, the one at the coffee shop, and decided…

Yes, she wanted him. Yes, she'd take this risk. Yes, she would put the past behind her and open her heart.

She wove her way through the city streets until the congestion eased and the roads opened up to an area filled with small office buildings and light industrial complexes. Her father's old building came into view, a squat one-story concrete building with a nondescript storefront and a long, rectangular shape. She sat there for a long moment, staring at the building, memorizing the sign. The Top Notch Printing sign had faded, and the white exterior paint that had once been so pristine had faded to a dingy gray. Weeds had sprung up between the cracks in the parking lot. The tidy building now looked sad, defeated.

It hit her then, hard and fast. She would never again drive up here and see Top Notch Printing on the front façade. Never again see the mailbox her father had painted himself one weekend. Never again walk through the door and hear her father call her name.

In the years since her father passed, no one had rented or bought the building, and it seemed to echo now with emptiness, disuse. Marnie parked, got out of the car, and flipped through the keys on her ring until she got to a brass one. The key had been on her father's ring for decades, and had a worn spot where his thumb had sat, morning after morning, when he opened the building for the day.

She slipped the key into the lock. The lock stuck a bit, then gave way, and the door opened with a creak. Once inside, her hand found the light switch, and the overhead fluorescents sputtered to life, providing a surreal white glow in the foyer. She stepped past the glass partition that divided the receptionist's desk from the main office. A smile curved across her face. Her father had never had a receptionist, but when the girls came in after school or on the weekends, they'd fought over sitting at that desk and answering the phones, as if it was the best job in the world.

Marnie ran a hand over the old corded desk phone, then let her gaze skip over the desk. Nothing there, or on the counter where her father would leave things for customers to pick up. She took a right, and headed down the hall, toward the big oak door that hadn't been opened in three years.

Her steps stuttered and she looked up at the engraved plaque attached to the oak.

TOM FRANKLIN

That was all, no title, nothing fancy. The guys in the shop had made the sign for him one day, and he'd mounted it with the caveat that they all called him Tom, just like always. He'd been a good boss, almost one of the guys, which had made his employees love him, but had often given them license to slack on production. Still, every person who had ever worked for her father came to his funeral, a testament to his memory, his lasting relationships with people. Tom had been a good guy, a good boss, and an even better father. Oh, how she missed him.

Marnie reached up, her fingers dancing over the engraved lettering. Then she tugged off the plaque and tucked it in her purse. Doing so left a scar on the door, which Marnie liked. It said Tom had been here, and shouldn't be forgotten.

A long, low creak announced the opening of the front door. Marnie wheeled around, raising her fist with the keys in it. Not much of a defense, but better than nothing. She lowered her fist when she saw a familiar figure enter the building. "Jack. You scared the heck out of me."

"Sorry." He stepped into the foyer, and his features shifted from shadows to light. In the white fluorescents, his eyes seemed even bluer, his hair darker, his jaw line sharper. Her heart started beating double-time. "I wanted to get here before you did, but I was running behind."

She took a step closer to him, letting the smile inside her bubble to the surface. "That's okay. You didn't have to be here. I could have picked this up myself."

He took a step closer, reached up a hand, and cupped her jaw, his gaze soft, tender. "Oh, Marnie, you are so determined to fly solo."

"It's safer that way," she whispered.

"But is it better?"

She shook her head, and tears rushed to her eyes. "No, it's not."

"Then stop doing it," he said. He smiled, then closed the distance between them and kissed her. This kiss was tender, gentle. His hands held her jaw, fingers tangling in her hair. She sighed into the kiss and leaned into Jack.

And it all felt so, so right. So perfect. Falling wasn't so bad, she realized. Not so bad at all.

Finally, Jack drew back, but didn't let her go, not right away. The connection between them tightened, as the threads they had been building began to knit into something real and lasting.

It was as if in that kiss, that moment of surrender, something fundamental had shifted between them. Marnie could feel it charging the air, the space between them. The grin playing on Jack's lips said he felt it, too. From here on out, nothing would be the same. And for the first time in her life, Marnie was ready to get on that roller coaster, but still, fear kept her from saying a word.

"Before we get too distracted, let me show you what I found. I put it on your father's desk." Jack reached past her, which whispered his cologne past her senses, and opened the door to Tom's office, allowing Marnie to enter first.

She took a deep breath, squared her shoulders, then went into the office. The second her feet touched the carpet, she jetted back in time. She hadn't been inside her father's office for years. At least four, maybe more. Once she'd gone off to college, then come home to open her own business, free time had become a rare commodity and her days of playing receptionist with her sisters had ended.

Nothing had changed with the passage of time. The worn black leather chair her father had rescued from a salvage sale still sat behind the simple dark green metal desk he'd painted himself. The bookshelf held a haphazard collection of business books—gifts, mostly—that he'd kept meaning to read and never had. A stack of print samples lay against one wall, and a dish of Tootsie Rolls sat on the corner of the desk, beside a hideous green pottery pen holder that Kat had made for Dad in the third grade. Marnie's throat swelled. "It's been three years and it still seems like I could walk in here and find him at his desk."

Jack put a hand on her shoulder. She leaned into his touch, allowed his stronger, broader shoulders to hold her up. "I'm sorry you lost him," he said. "He was a really nice guy."

"Yeah, he was." She stepped away from Jack's touch, and crossed to a box on the credenza behind the desk. Her name had been written across the top, in the same precise script as the note. Jack's handwriting. She danced a finger across the six letters of her name.

"I came across that when I was cleaning out the office," Jack said. "I thought you'd want to have it. For you and your sisters."

She pried open the cardboard. Instant recognition hit her, along with a teary wave of memories. She reached inside and pulled out the wooden photo frame, still filled with a picture of Dad and his girls, the three of them crowding the space in front of him. Ma had taken the picture, out in front of the building, years and years ago. Kat was about ten, Marnie almost nine and Erica just seven, the three of them wearing goofy smiles and matching pigtails. It wasn't the picture that caught her heart, though, it was the frame.

When her mother had brought home the print from the photo developer, Dad had showed it to Marnie and told her a special picture like this needed a special frame. He'd asked her to help him make one, and she'd leapt at the chance. Her father, who worked too many hours and came home to three girls all anxious for him to hear about school or help with homework or go outside to ride bikes, rarely had time to spend with just one daughter.

"My father and I made this together," she said, the memory slipping from her lips in a soft whisper. "He told the other girls that this was going to be a Dad and Daisy-doo project. Kat and Erica pouted, but Dad stuck to his guns. We went out to the garage, and he and I did everything, from cutting the wood to nailing the pieces together. He taught me how to miter the corners and sand the wood filler until it was smooth. When it was done—" she flipped over the frame and ran her fingers over the letters etched there "—he showed me how to use the woodburner to put our names on it."

And there, as deep and clear as the day she'd done it, were the words *Dad and His Daisy-Doo's Great Project.*

A great project, indeed. The best one, and one of the few things that had been just between her and her dad. Her throat clogged. Her vision blurred. *Oh, Dad.*

"I didn't even know he saved it." But of course he would have. Tom had been a sentimental man, who had held on to nearly every school paper his daughters brought home, framed the weekly drawings, and made a big deal out of every life event. Tears welled in her eyes, clung to her lashes. She clutched the frame to her chest. Solid, warm, it held so many memories. "Thank you."

"You're welcome." He let out a breath, then shifted his weight. His stance changed from commiseration to serious, and she knew this was something she might not want to hear. "I've got some things to tell you, Marnie, about the way I handled your father's business."

"It's okay. It's in the past. He's gone now."

"I know, but…this needs to be said. For both of us." Jack heaved a sigh. His gaze skipped around the room, coming to rest on the visitor's chair, as if he was sitting in it, across from her father again. "When I first met with your father, I came to him under false pretences. I promised him we'd help him. It was the same line we gave all the businesses we worked with. Sometimes, yes, we did help them, but sometimes we just invested and walked away, knowing they'd fail."

"How was that a smart strategy?"

Jack took a seat on the corner of the desk. "There's a lot that goes into a buying decision, you know? Pluses and minuses, current earnings versus future. Your father might not have been great at managing a business, but he was amazing at building customer relationships, and that meant his business had incredible future earning potential. Everybody loved the guy, loved working with him, and he had a great rapport with them. But..."

"But what?"

He heard the caution in Marnie's voice, and knew she was bracing herself for something she didn't want to hear. How he wanted to stop here, to not tell her anything. But the guilt had weighed on him heavy for years, and he couldn't keep seeing Marnie or ask anything more of her if she didn't know who he used to be.

"But there was a bigger company in town who wanted those same customers. They were a current client of my father's, and they had tried to buy your dad's business a few times, but he always refused."

"I vaguely remember something about that. My dad didn't talk about work very often."

"The competitor came to my father and I, asking us to go in, get Tom's business from him and then they could have the customers. There'd be a big bonus for Knight, of course, and a very happy client. At the time I thought it was the right thing to do. I justified it a hundred different ways. Your father was older, ready for retirement. He wasn't much of a businessman. He'd been talking about getting out of the company, having more time for himself. So I kept telling myself I was doing the right thing, that in the end, it was the best choice for Tom. But…"

Across from him, Marnie had gone cold and still. "But what?"

"But I liked your father. He was a great guy, like I said. The kind of guy you'd have a few beers with or split a pizza with. He was honest and forthright and nice."

"And trusting."

Jack nodded, hating himself for abusing that trust years ago. "And trusting."

"So you…" She clutched the frame between her hands, her knuckles whitening. "You threw him under the bus, for a bottom line?"

Jack sighed, and ran a hand through his hair. "Yes, I did all those things. I'm the one that talked to your father about Knight investing in his company. I'm the one that promised him we'd be there through thick and thin. And I'm the one who, in the end, deserted him. But, Marnie, there's more to it than what you know."

But she had already turned on her heel and headed out of the office. Before he could follow, she had rushed out. The door slammed in her wake.

Marnie ran. Her mind tried to process what Jack had told her, but it wouldn't compute. Jack had fed her father a line of lies. Then let him fail on purpose.

She jerked her keys out of her purse and thumbed the lock. A bright green pickup truck pulled into the lot.

The color triggered a memory in Marnie, and when the man in the truck got out, she remembered.

Doug Hendrickson, the twenty-something son of Floyd Hendrickson, who owned a rival printing company in Boston. Back in the early days of his business, Marnie's father and Floyd had worked together, helping each other build from the ground up, trading jobs, connections, equipment. Marnie could remember going into her father's shop on the weekends, and sometimes seeing Doug when he came in with his father.

Then Floyd and Tom had a falling out, over what Marnie had no idea, and the two had stopped speaking. They'd become fierce competitors then, each trying to grab their corner of the Boston printing market. She hadn't seen Floyd or his son in years, but she knew Doug's wide, friendly face in a second.

Doug cupped a hand over his brow to block the sun. "Is Jack around? I'm supposed to meet him here, but I'm early."

"You're meeting Jack? Jack Knight?" she said, instead of telling him Jack was right inside.

"Yup. You seen him?" Doug's gaze narrowed and he took a step closer. "Hey, aren't you Tom's daughter? Uh, Kat? Or…"

Marnie worked a smile to her face. "I'm the middle one. Marnie."

"I knew you looked familiar!" He grinned. "What a wicked small world. God, I haven't seen you in years. You're not thinking of reopening your dad's place, are you?"

She shook her head. "No."

The door opened behind her and Jack stepped into the sunshine. Damn. She should have left.

"Hey, Jack!" Doug greeted him with a smile. "Glad to see you. You got my check?"

Marnie jerked her gaze from one man to the other. "Check? What check?"

"Gee, Marnie, I would have thought someone would tell you." Doug put his hands in his back pockets and rocked on his heels. "I'm opening up my own shop. With some funding from my dad and Knight, of course. I met Jack here a few years ago and he set me up with this place and a nudge to go out on my own. This place was perfect because, well, it has all the equipment still. A little dusty, but it works." Then Doug seemed to realize what he'd said and his face sobered. "Sorry, Marnie. I know your dad passed and all, and this is probably hard."

She bit her lip. "Harder than you know. I'm glad you're the one giving this place a second life. I'm sorry if I seem short with you, Doug. It's just been a really tough day."

An ache started deep inside her chest and spread through Marnie, fast, painful, until she wanted to collapse, or run, or both. She had trusted Jack, opened her heart to him, begun to fall for him, and what did it get her? Hurt. Why had she taken that risk?

She spun toward Jack. "You did this?"

"It's complicated, Marnie. Your father—"

The anger and hurt inside her ignited. So many emotions, weeks' worth, really, bubbled to the surface. She'd kept it all tamped down, and now she wanted to explode, regardless of who was there or why. "You don't get to tell me anything more about my father. Or me. Or us. Or anything. Just leave me alone, Jack."

Before he could respond, she climbed into her car, started the engine and spun out of the parking lot. Tears blurred her vision, but she swiped them away and drove hard and fast, away from a huge mistake she'd almost made.

Just when she'd begun to think that Jack Knight was a good man, just when she was about to give him a chance, to trust that the man she'd seen at the gym and the coffee shop and the charity was the real Jack, he did something like this.

Sold the remains of her father's company to his competitor. Just like the vulture she knew he was all along.

CHAPTER TWELVE

HE SHOULD HAVE let her go. She was hurting, and like a wounded animal, Marnie wanted to escape from the person she saw as responsible for her pain. She had left the office, and run for the car, dodging the rain that had started to fall again. Her tires squealed against the pavement, spitting gravel in her wake, and then she was gone.

Jack hesitated for a half a second, shouted a *meet you later* at Doug, then he hopped in his car and wove through the traffic, darting left, right, until he saw her gray sedan ahead. He pulled in behind her, following as she navigated the city, driving against the tide of outbound traffic.

She passed her office, took a left instead of the right that would have brought her to her mother's house, and passed by the exit for her condo. She turned down Charles Street, then entered the Boston Common Parking Garage. Jack found a space a half level above her, then hopped out in time to see Marnie heading up the stairs and out one of the parking kiosks located on the Common. She crossed Charles, then entered the Public Garden. He lingered behind, warring with letting her go and running after her. Hadn't he hurt her enough? Done enough damage?

She headed down the wide sidewalk that led to the pond and the swan boat rides. For a moment, he thought maybe that was her destination—a quiet ride on the tranquil pond while swans and ducks bobbed nearby, begging for crumbs. But her steps slowed, then stopped. She took a seat on a bench. When he saw the hunch in her shoulders, the decision was made for him. He couldn't let her hurt for one more second. Because—

Because he was falling in love with Marnie Franklin. Hell, he'd been falling for her ever since they'd met. It had been those shoes, those impractical, uncomfortable shoes that she'd kicked onto the pavement. A barefoot Cinderella who had enticed him with her fiery hair and her feisty attitude.

She might never forgive him, and might hate him for the rest of her life, but that didn't mean he wasn't going to try to rectify the mess he had made years ago. And maybe, just maybe, he'd find some peace finally. He might not be able to fix this enough to allow him and Marnie to be together, but maybe he could make it better for her.

He sat down on the space beside her on the bench. Her eyes widened with surprise. "Let me guess," he said, gesturing to the statue across from them, "favorite book as a child?"

Instead of answering, she wheeled on him. "Why are you here, Jack?"

"Because I'm trying to explain to you what happened."

"You can't. It's too late." Her eyes misted and she turned away, facing the bronze statues across the walkway. A mother duck, followed by several baby ducks, waddled from the nest to the pond. The statues were a Boston Public Garden landmark, based on the famous

Robert McCloskey book about a family of ducks who had battled city traffic and rushing bicycles to settle in this very park.

"That's the statues based on *Make Way for Ducklings,* right?" he said, because he didn't know what else to say. Far easier to focus on some metal ducks than on climbing the wall between himself and Marnie. "That book's a classic."

"My father gave me the book for Christmas when I was a little girl." She turned to him, the anger still in her green eyes, the hurt rising in the bloom of her cheeks. "Do you want to know why?"

"Yes, I do." He wanted to know everything about Marnie, to memorize every detail of this intriguing woman who named flowers and blushed at the drop of a hat.

She bit her lip, then exhaled, but the tears still shone in her eyes. "Because he said no matter how far any of us girls got from him, he'd always be there to make sure we got home okay. He said he'd be there." She stopped, drawing in a breath, then letting it out again with a powerful sigh. "And he's not there. Not now, not ever again. Because of you and your investment. You ruined our lives, Jack, and because of that, he just gave up and…died."

Jack let out a long breath and rested his arms on his knees. "I know I did. And I'm sorry."

She sat beside him, still as the statues. "I don't understand, Jack. You helped Dot and your friend with the gym, and Luanne and Harvey. Why not my father? Why wasn't he worth you doing the same as you did for them?"

Jack's gaze rested on the bronze ducklings, forever frozen in their quest to tag along after their parents.

"When I went to work for my
a relationship with him. I thougl
him, then he'd, I don't know, sta
me an attaboy at least. So I learne
I mastered them, and I went in the
burn and fire sale approach, and did
He let out a curse. "I destroyed cor
off like stolen car parts, and waited f to say
I'd done a good job. He never did. He found fault where there was none, complained about my soft heart when I didn't pull the funding plug fast enough…" Jack threw up his hands. "There was no winning with that man. He was committed to the bottom line and nothing else."

"And my father's business was part of that bottom line? Because it meant more to your father gone than working?"

"Yes." Saying it to Marnie's face hurt Jack far more than speaking to any of the other business owners in that pile of folders on his desk. He wished he could undo the past, flip a switch, and change everything. "Every time I did what my father asked me to do, I died a little inside. I was so caught up in the thrill of it all, the hunt, the chase, the capture, that I couldn't see the impact on the people, or on me."

Marnie just listened.

"When I met your father, and convinced him to sign with us," Jack said, "I liked him. A lot. And for the first time, I felt like the lowest level of scum there was because I knew I was lying and I knew what was going to happen to his business. I realized what I'd been doing and how it had turned me into someone I didn't even like, someone who lied to get what he wanted, who toed the company line no matter what it cost other people. After that, I quit working for my father. I walked away.

me a couple weeks to find another job, and in at time, my dad went to your father and told him there was no hope. Nothing to salvage. He convinced your father to sign over the rest of the company to Knight."

"For pennies on the dollar."

Jack nodded. "By the time my father died and I was in that president's chair, it was too late. Your father had left, and didn't want to come back to the business." He still remembered that morning meeting with Tom Franklin. Regrets had haunted Jack for years. He'd been too late, then and now. Too damned late.

"Wait. You offered my father his company back?"

"His was one of the first I tried to fix. It was the one I wanted most to save, but your dad was done, and I think, glad to be out of the chief's role. He said he loved the industry, but hated the stress of being an owner. He seemed…relieved when I talked to him. I kept trying. I called him every week. But he kept saying no. Said he wanted to be retired and enjoy what time he had left. So I stopped."

"What do you mean, what time he had left?"

"He didn't tell you?"

"Tell me what?"

Oh, hell. Jack hesitated. He looked into Marnie's wide green eyes, and wondered if deep inside her, she already knew what he was going to say. "Your father had a heart condition. He'd known about it for years and I think that's what really drove him to get investors, to try to take some of the stress off his shoulders. After I lost my dad from the same thing, I tried to encourage Tom to get to the doctor, listen to the medical advice, but he was…" Jack's voice trailed off.

"A proud and stubborn man." She let out a gust and jerked to her feet. For a moment, she fumed, then she nodded. "My mother had hinted at this. That my father wanted time, and that she wanted him to have it, too. They knew. But they kept it from us."

"He didn't want you to worry, I'm sure. That's why he kept this all secret."

"Secrets are how people get hurt!" The words exploded out of her and she turned away. "If that's love, I don't want it." She waved a hand, as if brushing away a wasp. "Leave it for everyone else."

He stepped to the side, until she looked up at him again. In her face, he saw the scared woman buried deep inside her. So afraid to trust. That had been him, too, for much too long. No more. If he kept letting fear rule his heart, he was going to miss out on someone incredible. Marnie.

"Marnie, your father *did* love you girls and your mother," Jack said. "He talked about you all like his family was the best in the world. He was trying to protect you all, right or wrong."

After a long moment, realization and acceptance dawned in Marnie's eyes. "Because then we'd want to help. We'd want to talk about it. And if there's one thing my family excelled at, it was not talking about anything." She cursed and shook her head, then wrapped her arms around herself, even though the day was warm. "My whole life was like that. Things happening beyond my control. My father would keep his business worries to himself, play the jokester, the happy guy, my mother would act like everything was perfect, and I'd feel like I was missing something. Something necessary and important."

Jack rose and took her hand in his. "Oh, Marnie, I'm sure they didn't do it to hurt you."

"But it did all the same. And so I grew up, and I decided I'd control everything I could. And do the same for them. Protect my mother from…you. From love, from happiness."

"From me?"

"I was afraid that if she saw you, she'd remember what had happened to my father and be hurt all over again. But really, I was just looking for a reason to stay away from this…risk between us." She bit her lip, and finally admitted the truth to herself. Her father had lost his business and her world had been thrust into chaos. Then he died, and the chaos got worse. Both things happened outside her realm of control, and had only made her dig her heels in further. "I have my lists and my organizational things and it all gives me comfort. I went into a business where I can control people's happy endings. And you know what?" She lifted her gaze to his, and felt tears fill her eyes. "Control hasn't made me any happier. It's made me scared and reluctant. And left me alone. The only match I can't make is the one for myself, because falling in love means letting go. Taking a chance. Trusting another person. And maybe getting hurt in the process."

Jack danced his fingers along her cheek. "And would that be so bad?"

She nodded, scared even now. A part of her wanted to hold on to the comfort of that fear, but she had done that for far too long and ended up running from Jack, running from the truth, and most of all, running from the very thing she wanted.

Love.

Her gaze went to the statues again and she realized her father may not have told her everything, but in his own way, he'd always been trying to prepare his daughters for the end. "Whenever he read *Make Way for Ducklings* to me, my father used to add an epilogue. He would tell me that there would be a day when Mr. and Mrs. Mallard could no longer lead the way for the ducklings to go to the little island, and that the ducklings shouldn't worry. When that day came, that was when the ducklings knew it was time for them to spread their wings and find their own ponds. He said the Mallards knew their ducklings would be fine because they were smart and strong and would always have the love of their parents at their backs." The tears slid down her cheeks now, dropping onto her hands and glistening in the fading light. What she wouldn't give to hear him tell that story one more time. "He wanted me and my sisters to find our own ponds and not to worry about him."

"Because you are smart and strong and would always have his love."

She nodded, mute, and the tears fell, and Jack pulled her into his chest, holding her tight and strong. She cried for a long time, while pigeons cooed at their feet and the sun began to set over Boston. She cried and his heart broke for her, and he wished that of all the things he had fixed, that he could fix this one most of all. She cried and Jack envied her father, and hoped Tom Franklin knew how lucky he had been to have people love him like this.

Finally, Marnie drew back and swiped at her eyes. "I'm sorry."

He whisked away one more tear with his thumb, then cupped her jaw. "Don't be. I'm sorry I didn't stand up to my father sooner. I'm sorry I wasn't here when your father needed me most. I'm sorry I didn't tell you all of this sooner. I'm sorry for a thousand things, and a thousand more. I've been trying to make it up to the people my father's company destroyed ever since that day, because that's the only thing that's going to let me sleep at night. I can't change the past, but hopefully I can make the future better."

"And the Hendricksons? Are they part of that?"

Jack shook his head. "That was all your father's idea. He said he wanted to see the next generation carry the company forward. He told me to contact Doug and tell him that after he got out of college, he could buy the building and its contents for a fair price."

"You held on to that property all this time? Because my father asked you to?"

Jack nodded. "It was the least I could do." He brushed back the lock of hair that had fallen across her brow. "I'm sorry, Marnie."

It was as if he couldn't say the words enough. She was the face of his and his father's selfish decisions, the mirror Jack looked into every day. But telling her and getting the truth on the table, as painful as it had been, had eased the guilt in his chest. For the first time since he'd taken a seat behind his father's desk, he felt as if he'd made a difference. Like he could stop beating himself up for the past.

"I'm glad you're helping Doug. I truly am. I couldn't think of a single soul that would take better care of my father's dream." She gave him a grateful smile. "My mother told me once that my father said he thought you were a good man when he met you."

"Really?" Jack thought of who he had been, and couldn't imagine why Tom would say such a thing.

"One of my father's skills, and I think it's something I inherited and use in my matchmaking, is seeing the best in people. He knew who you were inside, and that's what he saw. That's all he saw. That's why he trusted you."

Jack shook his head. "He must have had a crystal ball into the future because I sure wasn't a good man back then."

"But now, you are."

"Now I'm just trying to make up for the past. Going into the same office, day after day, and trying to undo the damage." He shrugged. "I'm not sure that makes me good or bad, more…doing my job."

She thought about that for a second as a trio of bicyclers sped past them, and a family paused to admire the bronze ducklings. The end of the day brought more people to the park, their voices rising and falling like music.

"You know, you and I are a lot alike," Marnie said. "We both keep taking comfort in the things we know, the things we can rein in, rather than risk it all for the unknown. It's like what you said in your speech about taking chances. It's so much easier, isn't it, not to confront, not to upset? It's just another way to control the situation. When really—" at this, she let out a little laugh "—the one you're really not confronting is yourself. Your own fears and insecurities and worries."

How right she was. He'd gone along with his father's plans for years, because he didn't want to look in the mirror at what he'd been doing. And now, he'd avoided relationships under the guise of not wanting to repeat his family history, rather than looking at the inner demons that kept him from making a commitment. He took her hand, letting his thumb rub across the back of her fingers. Her hand felt good in his, right. "All we can do, as my stepfather says, is to live and learn, and do things different going forward."

She nodded. "That's good advice, Jack. You should take it."

"I'm trying." He grinned.

"I mean it. You should go after the things you're afraid of."

"I'm trying to go after you." He moved closer, reaching for her, but she stepped out of his grasp. "But you keep running away from me."

He reached up and cupped her jaw. He could look at her face every day for the rest of his life. Hear her say his name every morning and night, forever. After his engagement ended, he'd been afraid to risk his heart, and it almost cost him this woman. His stepfather had been right. He had been scared, terrified really, of opening his heart to Marnie because it meant taking a risk that he could turn out like his father. He was done with that. Done with worrying. The best thing to do—

Take the leap anyway.

Jack let his thumb trail along her bottom lip. "All that fire and sass, in one woman. No wonder I can't stop thinking about you."

She shook her head. "Don't, Jack. Don't do this."

She was going to bolt, and he didn't know how to stop that. Despite her words, the woman who brought people together for a living still lived in fear of her own happy ending, held that fear like a security blanket. He and Marnie were so alike, he thought, burned by their pasts and using their jobs to cover for their emotions.

"Don't what, fall in love with you? Too late, Marnie."

She swallowed hard and her eyes widened. "But we've only known each other a few weeks and we barely dated or anything."

"When you know, you know. Doesn't that happen to your clients all the time?"

"Yes, but this is different."

"How?"

"It just is."

He wanted to shake her, to tell her to take down that stubborn wall, and open her heart. But he knew she would do that only when she was ready. Pushing her would only push her away, the last thing he wanted.

His gaze dropped to her lips, trembling with the fear still in her heart, then raised his gaze to her eyes, wide, cautious. "Why are you so terrified of the very thing you tell everyone else in the world to go after?"

"I…I'm not." The lie flushed her cheeks.

"Do you know why my engagement ended?" Jack said. "Tanya left me because she said I was cold. Uninvolved. More interested in work than in our relationship. I lost her, and it was all my fault. I've kept my heart closed off ever since, and worked myself half to death, because I thought that was easier. After all, I learned that art from the master." He let out a gust and a low curse. "The irony of the whole thing is that the one man I never wanted to emulate—my father—was the man I had started to become. I won't make that mistake again, nor am I going to spend one more day alone just because I'm afraid of his legacy. I'm done running from relationships. The question is—" he took her hand again "—are you?"

"You think I'm running? Look in the mirror, Jack. You're afraid, too."

"I'm not afraid of anything, Marnie."

"Really? You told Luanne that you originally went to college to be a writer, then changed your major to business. Why? Because you wanted to make your father happy, not you. You told me yourself that you don't love your job, and you had thought about doing something else, but put it off. My question for you is why are you still working in your father's business if your first love was in writing?"

He scoffed. "Any business person will tell you that a job like that, where the sales and return on investment are almost completely out of your hands, is crazy. I've read the statistics. I know how many writers are making poverty level wages, and how many—"

"Are talking themselves out of it because they're afraid. Stop investing in other people, Jack, and invest in yourself. Then maybe…" Her green eyes met his, soft, vulnerable. "Maybe we can be."

Now she did leave, and this time, he didn't follow her. He sat back down on the bench and watched the bronze ducks marching on a perpetual journey to lands unknown. And wondered how a smart man could be so very, very stupid.

Marnie stood at her thirty-first wedding of the year and tried like heck to look happy. Instead, she suspected she had a face fit for a funeral. She shifted on her heels, slipped a glance at her watch, and bit back a groan. She'd only been here for five minutes. She couldn't make a decent exit until at least thirty minutes had passed.

This was what she worked so hard for, this was the icing on the matchmaking cake, and all the other times, she loved the moment when she saw a couple she had brought together pledge to be together forever. But not this time.

Not since Jack.

She hadn't taken any of his calls. Had refused the flowers he'd sent over. He'd even sent over a first edition of *Make Way for Ducklings,* with a little note inside that said:

The only way to get to the right pond is to take the risk and cross the street. Love, Jack.

That one word had scared her spitless, and she'd tucked the book on a shelf. Erica had just shook her head and not said anything. Marnie buried herself with work, staying late and getting to the office early, making matches until her head hurt.

Late at night, Marnie faced the truth. She was doing it again. Running from her own fears. Rather than confronting them. Was she always going to be like this? Afraid to take the very risks she encouraged her clients to take?

Her sisters and her mother had taken a leap of faith when it came to love. All three were happy as could be, and yet Marnie held back. Why?

She stood to the side of the room, watching couples kiss and dance, while the bride and groom waltzed to their favorite song. Marnie stood alone, flying solo, like she did at most of these events. And feeling miserable.

She had thought, when she walked out of the park, that she was doing the right thing. But really, she had been retreating again. All the emotions of the last few days had overwhelmed her, and brought her deepest fears roaring to the surface. So much for that resolve to go ahead and fall for Jack.

Okay, she had done that. She had fallen for him when he named the daisy Fred. But acting on those feelings—

That terrified her.

Jack had told her that people live and learn and then try to do things different going forward. Thus far, all she'd done was stick to her comfort zone. Which sure as heck wasn't keeping her warm at night.

Wedding guests tapped their forks against their wine glasses, the musical sound signaling to the bride and groom to kiss. Marnie watched Janet and Mark Shalvis giggle, then join hands and kiss each other, happiness exuding from them like perfume.

She thought of the cookie crumbs. The daisies. The picnic. The rain storm. Then she glanced in the mirror on the wall, and saw a woman who made her living creating happy endings, and had to make one of her own.

What was she waiting for? Was she going to be at her thirty-second wedding, still alone, still wishing she'd gone after what she wanted?

The only way to get to the right pond is to take the risk and cross the street.

Even if she didn't know what waited for her on the other side of the street. Or if he still wanted her. But if she didn't do it now, she'd always regret not acting, and Marnie Franklin was tired, dog tired, of living with regrets. If there was one thing her father's death should have taught her, it was that life was short. Her mother had moved on and found happiness in her golden years. What was Marnie waiting for?

Marnie drew in a deep breath, then strode across the room, over to the newly married couple. "Congratulations, you guys. I hate to leave, but I really have to go."

Janet pouted. "Can't you stay a little while longer? I really wanted to introduce you to my mom. And I have three single cousins who could use your help. They're like an advertisement for a lonely hearts club."

How tempting it would be to retreat to that default position of work, instead of risk. For a second Marnie considered it. After all, what difference would a day make?

No. She'd wasted enough days already. She shook her head, and gave Janet a smile. "Have them call me tomorrow. Right now, I have to go. I have a very important match to go make. This one needs…my personal touch."

Janet took her arm and gave it a gentle squeeze. "Good. Because no one knows what's right for another's heart like you do, Marnie."

Even her own, she thought, as she waved goodbye and hurried out the door of the ballroom. The need to be out of here, to be across town, filled her, and she couldn't move fast enough. Her heels slowed her steps, and she kicked them off, gathering them up by the straps and running barefoot across the tiled lobby. Once outside the hotel, she raised her arm to call a cab, when that familiar silver sports car glided into the spot beside her. Dare she hope?

The window on the passenger's side rolled down. "I really need to take you shoe shopping."

The deep voice thrilled her, lifted her heart. He was here. Had he read her mind? Or did he have business inside the hotel? She bent down and saw Jack's familiar grin in the driver's side. "What are you doing here?"

"Rescuing Cinderella before the clock strikes midnight." He leaned over and opened the door. "Do you need a ride to the ball?"

"Actually, I'm leaving the ball," she said, then got inside the car and shut the door. "I was going to go look for the prince. But it appears he already found me. How on earth did you do that in a city this size?"

"Bloodhounds." He grinned. "No, I'm kidding. You wouldn't talk to me. I got desperate. So I bribed your sister to tell me where you were."

"You bribed Erica?"

"It's amazing what kind of information a chocolate cupcake can buy." Jack chuckled, then put the car in gear and pulled away from the curb. A light rain started up, casting the city in shades of gray, and reminding Marnie of that afternoon at the jazz festival. "If you hadn't come out of that wedding, I would have ended up making quite a scene."

"Oh, really? And what would you have done?"

Jack turned into an empty parking lot, stopped the car and turned to Marnie. The rain fell faster now, pattering against the glass, the roof. "I had it all planned out. I was going to march in there, daisies blazing—" he reached into the back seat and pulled out a huge spray of white daisies "—and tell the entire world that I loved you."

Joy bubbled in her heart. Once, those words would have filled her with fear, but no more. She'd almost lost him, and that realization had woken her up to the fact that she took this chance now, or lost it forever. She thumbed in the direction they'd just come. "You know, we can always go back."

"Maybe later," he said, then put the daisies on the dash and pulled her to him. "After I'm done kissing you."

She put up a hand to stop him. "Wait. I need to tell you something first."

He drew back, hurt shimmering in his eyes. "Okay. Shoot."

"I told you that you weren't facing your fears, when really, I should have said that to myself. It's just that finding out all that stuff about my father, just kicked me in the gut, and so I retreated to my default position." She let out a gust. "I buried my head in the sand, which is exactly what I blamed my parents for doing for years. Ironic, isn't it? That I did the very thing I hated?"

"Sometimes we repeat what we know, even if we don't realize it at the time."

"I put off confronting you and told myself it was because I didn't want to hurt my mother. But really, I was afraid of looking at *me.* At how I was starting to feel for you, and how much that scared me. I let what happened with my father be the reason to avoid a relationship with you because I was damned afraid of letting go."

"And now?"

"Now, I…" She paused, and the smile inside her heart made its way to her face. "Now I just ditched my clients because I wanted to run across town and tell you how I felt."

When he returned the smile, that zing ran through her, faster and more powerful than ever before. If she'd been a matchmaker with a client, she would have told the client to listen to that zing. To follow its lead. Because it always led to the heart's true desire. She raised her lips to Jack's. "I'm falling for you, Jack. You came into my life with a bang, and scared the hell out of me because you kept trying to get me to let my hair down, to be spontaneous and fun and *unfettered.*" She laughed again at the word he'd used to describe her.

He brushed her bangs away from her eyes with two gentle fingers. "You are damned sexy that way, you know."

"Oh, really?" She grinned, then released her curls from the clip that held them in place. Her crimson hair cascaded onto her shoulders.

Jack let out a groan and pulled her closer. "We have got to get out of this car and behind a closed door, because I am not making the same mistake I did in the parking lot." His blue eyes darkened with desire and he leaned toward her.

"Wait. There's one other thing." She bit her lip and

feigned a serious look. "Before you and I go any further, I wanted to set you up on one more match."

He groaned. "Marnie, I don't want to—"

"She's a redhead. Who loves daisies and has this silly habit of naming the flowers she receives. She loves jazz music and peanut butter cookies, and doesn't mind running through the rain, even if she often wears completely impractical shoes." Jack grinned and leaned in closer, but Marnie put up a finger and pressed it to his lips. "I have to warn you. She's complicated and scared as hell of having her heart broken. But that hasn't stopped this reluctant Cinderella from falling in love with a prince in a silver sports car."

"She sounds like the perfect match for me." The words danced across her fingers, followed by a quick, light kiss. His blue eyes lit with a teasing light. "Though she may want to think twice about getting tangled up with that prince. He's a business owner who's writing a book in his spare time. A guy who has made a few bad choices, but is doing his damnedest to make up for them. And before you get too sold on him, you should know he hates romantic comedies but loves action movies."

She shook her head. "Oh, that could be a deal breaker."

He chuckled, then drew Marnie into his arms. "Maybe we'll just watch the news instead."

"Or," she said, and a delicious smile curved up her face, "we could stay in bed and not watch anything."

"Now *that* sounds like a plan." Jack kissed her then, a deep, sweet, tender kiss that soared in Marnie's veins and filled her heart to the brim. She'd taken the risk, and found exactly what she was looking for on the other side—

Her own happy ending. And as she kissed Jack, the

rain fell and the city rushed by in its busy way. But inside the car, the world had slowed to just the two of them, and the match made in heaven.

Three months later, Marnie and Jack stood at the thirty-second wedding of the year, and by far, the biggest success story for Matchmaking by Marnie. From the minute she walked down the aisle, between Dan and Helen, Jack hadn't been able to take his eyes off Marnie. She had to be the most beautiful bride he'd ever seen. She had her hair down, that riot of red curls a stark, sexy contrast to the simple satin sheath dress she wore.

"I love you, Mrs. Knight," he whispered in her ear. They were sitting at the banquet table, with her sisters on either side, while several dozen of their friends enjoyed the food and music. It had been a simple wedding, held outside on the grassy lawn of a country club, with white table and chair sets and a small portable dance floor. Beside them was a small pond, with a pair of ducks making lazy circles through the water. Nothing too fancy, nothing too elaborate. But a day he knew he'd never forget. The summer sun shone over them, like it was smiling down on their happiness. The weatherman had predicted a storm, but so far, everything had been perfect.

"I love you, too, Mr. Knight." She grinned up at him, and Jack thought there was no sight more beautiful in the world than his wife's smile. *His wife.*

He didn't know if he'd ever get used to how amazing that sounded. He hoped not. He owed that cab driver a thank-you for being a distracted driver that night.

"I hope you're ready to dance tonight," Marnie said.

"Always, if it's with you. Though it depends on what you're wearing for shoes, Cinderella."

She chuckled, then lifted the hem of her dress to reveal very sensible and very comfortable decorated tennis shoes. They'd been studded with rhinestones and featured lacy bows. He laughed. Leave it to Marnie to surprise him, even today.

"I didn't want anything to spoil our wedding," she said.

"Nothing would spoil today, not even a freak winter storm," he said, then kissed her. She curved into his arms, a perfect fit. She had been, from the first moment he met her.

"Oh! My! God! You guys are the cutest couple ever! I can't believe you invited me to your wedding!" The high, loud voice of Roberta carried across the lawn, rising several decibels above the music and the murmurs of the guests. Jack and Marnie laughed, then turned toward her. She sent them a wave, then got back to shimmying her bright pink clad self with Hector on the dance floor. The couple had been together for several months now, and had even talked about marriage. A miracle, in Marnie's eyes.

"I think she's finally found her match," Marnie whispered to Jack. "I owe you big time for introducing them. I was worried I'd never find a match for Roberta."

"Oh, and I intend to collect on that debt. For the rest of our lives." He leaned in and kissed his wife, while guests clinked their glasses and cheered them on.

The DJ shifted the music from a fast song to a slow, romantic song. Couples began to head for the dance floor, including her sisters and their dates. Jack put out his hand for Marnie.

There was a rumble, and an instant later, the skies opened up, dropping a fast, furious, soaking summer storm. Guests began to run toward the building, shrieking in the rain, and hurrying to keep from getting wet. The dance floor emptied out, the DJ pulled the plug and dashed inside, yelling that his equipment would be ruined. Even Roberta and Hector made a fast break for the cover of the country club. But Marnie stayed where she was with Jack.

"Don't you want to get inside?" he said.

She shook her head, even as little rivers of water ran down her cheeks and arms. Her dress was already plastered to her body, but she didn't seem to care. "They say that a little rain is lucky on your wedding day. And I want to make sure we have all the luck we need."

"Oh, Marnie, we already do," Jack said softly and drew her to him. "We have each other."

They kissed again, while the ducks quacked and the rain fell and the world around them dropped away. They kissed until the storm abated and the sun came out again, as if giving their marriage its own blessing. They kissed, and for the first time in their lives, Jack and Marnie put their faith in happily ever after.

* * * * *

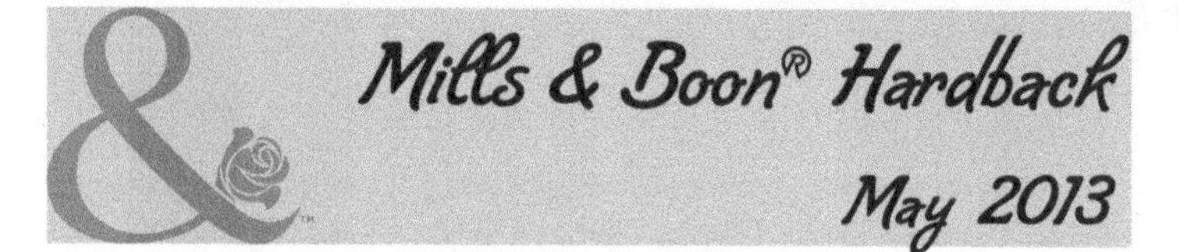

ROMANCE

A Rich Man's Whim	Lynne Graham
A Price Worth Paying?	Trish Morey
A Touch of Notoriety	Carole Mortimer
The Secret Casella Baby	Cathy Williams
Maid for Montero	Kim Lawrence
Captive in his Castle	Chantelle Shaw
Heir to a Dark Inheritance	Maisey Yates
A Legacy of Secrets	Carol Marinelli
Her Deal with the Devil	Nicola Marsh
One More Sleepless Night	Lucy King
A Father for Her Triplets	Susan Meier
The Matchmaker's Happy Ending	Shirley Jump
Second Chance with the Rebel	Cara Colter
First Comes Baby...	Michelle Douglas
Anything but Vanilla...	Liz Fielding
It was Only a Kiss	Joss Wood
Return of the Rebel Doctor	Joanna Neil
One Baby Step at a Time	Meredith Webber

MEDICAL

NYC Angels: Flirting with Danger	Tina Beckett
NYC Angels: Tempting Nurse Scarlet	Wendy S. Marcus
One Life Changing Moment	Lucy Clark
P.S. You're a Daddy!	Dianne Drake

0413 GEN STD HB

ROMANCE

Beholden to the Throne	Carol Marinelli
The Petrelli Heir	Kim Lawrence
Her Little White Lie	Maisey Yates
Her Shameful Secret	Susanna Carr
The Incorrigible Playboy	Emma Darcy
No Longer Forbidden?	Dani Collins
The Enigmatic Greek	Catherine George
The Heir's Proposal	Raye Morgan
The Soldier's Sweetheart	Soraya Lane
The Billionaire's Fair Lady	Barbara Wallace
A Bride for the Maverick Millionaire	Marion Lennox

HISTORICAL

Some Like to Shock	Carole Mortimer
Forbidden Jewel of India	Louise Allen
The Caged Countess	Joanna Fulford
Captive of the Border Lord	Blythe Gifford
Behind the Rake's Wicked Wager	Sarah Mallory

MEDICAL

Maybe This Christmas...?	Alison Roberts
A Doctor, A Fling & A Wedding Ring	Fiona McArthur
Dr Chandler's Sleeping Beauty	Melanie Milburne
Her Christmas Eve Diamond	Scarlet Wilson
Newborn Baby For Christmas	Fiona Lowe
The War Hero's Locked-Away Heart	Louisa George

0413 GEN STD LP

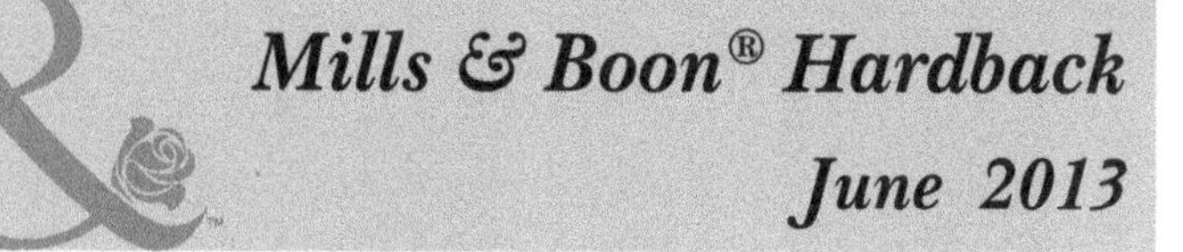

ROMANCE

The Sheikh's Prize	Lynne Graham
Forgiven but not Forgotten?	Abby Green
His Final Bargain	Melanie Milburne
A Throne for the Taking	Kate Walker
Diamond in the Desert	Susan Stephens
A Greek Escape	Elizabeth Power
Princess in the Iron Mask	Victoria Parker
An Invitation to Sin	Sarah Morgan
Too Close for Comfort	Heidi Rice
The Right Mr Wrong	Natalie Anderson
The Making of a Princess	Teresa Carpenter
Marriage for Her Baby	Raye Morgan
The Man Behind the Pinstripes	Melissa McClone
Falling for the Rebel Falcon	Lucy Gordon
Secrets & Saris	Shoma Narayanan
The First Crush Is the Deepest	Nina Harrington
One Night She Would Never Forget	Amy Andrews
When the Cameras Stop Rolling...	Connie Cox

MEDICAL

NYC Angels: Making the Surgeon Smile	Lynne Marshall
NYC Angels: An Explosive Reunion	Alison Roberts
The Secret in His Heart	Caroline Anderson
The ER's Newest Dad	Janice Lynn

0513 GEN STD HB